"Thank you for being a gentleman and walking me to my door," Moira said.

Shaw shrugged away her words. She laughed and, one heel still acting as a doorstop, she raised herself slightly on her toes and brushed her lips against his cheek.

The light touch of skin against skin instantly aroused him, placing Shaw on automatic pilot before he quite realized what was happening.

She drew her head back and looked up at him, her eyes staring into his soul. Had he been thinking clearly, he would have taken the opportunity to leave.

But he wasn't.

He didn't.

Instead, he took her into his arms and lowered his mouth to hers as if it had been written somewhere that he should. As if it had been scripted....

Dear Reader,

Well, June may be the traditional month for weddings, but we here at Silhouette find June is busting out all over—with babies! We begin with Christine Rimmer's *Fifty Ways To Say I'm Pregnant.* When bound-for-the-big-city Starr Bravo shares a night of passion with the rancher she's always loved, she finds herself in the family way. But how to tell him? *Fifty Ways* is a continuation of Christine's Bravo Family saga, so look for the BRAVO FAMILY TIES flash. And for those of you who remember Christine's JONES GANG series, you'll be delighted with the cameo appearance of an old friend....

Next, Joan Elliott Pickart continues her miniseries THE BABY BET: MACALLISTER'S GIFTS with *Accidental Family,* the story of a day-care center worker and a single dad with amnesia who find themselves falling for each other as she cares for their children together. And there's another CAVANAUGH JUSTICE offering in Special Edition from Marie Ferrarella: in *Cavanaugh's Woman,* an actress researching a film role needs a top cop—and Shaw Cavanaugh fits the bill nicely. *Hot August Nights* by Christine Flynn continues THE KENDRICKS OF CAMELOT miniseries, in which the reserved, poised Kendrick daughter finds her one-night stand with the town playboy coming back to haunt her in a big way. Janis Reams Hudson begins MEN OF CHEROKEE ROSE with *The Daddy Survey,* in which two little girls go all out to get their mother a new husband. And don't miss *One Perfect Man,* in which almost-new author Lynda Sandoval tells the story of a career-minded events planner who has never had time for romance until she gets roped into planning a party for the daughter of a devastatingly handsome single father. So enjoy the rising temperatures, all six of these wonderful romances...and don't forget to come back next month for six more, in Silhouette Special Edition.

Happy Reading!

Gail Chasan
Senior Editor

Marie Ferrarella

CAVANAUGH'S WOMAN

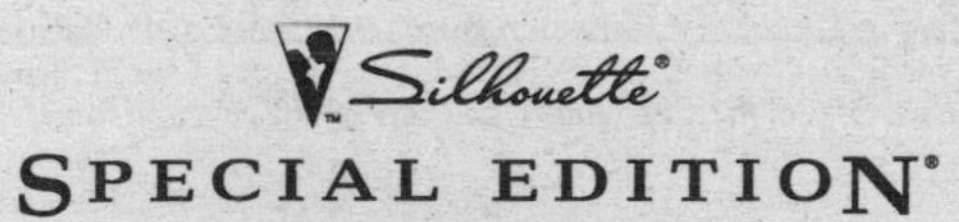

Published by Silhouette Books
America's Publisher of Contemporary Romance

To
Nancy Parodi Neubert
and
a friendship that goes back to
elementary school

SILHOUETTE BOOKS

ISBN 0-373-24617-X

CAVANAUGH'S WOMAN

This edition published by arrangement with Harlequin Books S.A.

Visit Silhouette Books at www.eHarlequin.com

Printed in U.S.A.

Books by Marie Ferrarella in Miniseries

ChildFinders, Inc.
A Hero for All Seasons IM #932
A Forever Kind of Hero IM #943
Hero in the Nick of Time IM #956
Hero for Hire IM #1042
An Uncommon Hero Silhouette Books
A Hero in Her Eyes IM #1059
Heart of a Hero IM #1105

Baby's Choice
Caution: Baby Ahead SR #1007
Mother on the Wing SR #1026
Baby Times Two SR #1037

The Baby of the Month Club
Baby's First Christmas SE #997
Happy New Year—Baby! IM #686
The 7lb., 2oz. Valentine Yours Truly
Husband: Optional SD #988
Do You Take This Child? SR #1145
Detective Dad World's Most Eligible Bachelors
The Once and Future Father IM #1017
In the Family Way Silhouette Books
Baby Talk Silhouette Books
An Abundance of Babies SE #1422

Like Mother, Like Daughter
One Plus One Makes Marriage SR #1328
Never Too Late for Love SR #1351

The Bachelors of Blair Memorial
In Graywolf's Hands IM #1155
M.D. Most Wanted IM #1167
Mac's Bedside Manner SE #1492
Undercover M.D. IM #1191

Two Halves of a Whole
The Baby Came C.O.D. SR #1264
Desperately Seeking Twin Yours Truly

***The Reeds**
Callaghan's Way IM #601
Serena McKee's Back in Town IM #808

Those Sinclairs
Holding Out for a Hero IM #496
Heroes Great and Small IM #501
Christmas Every Day IM #538
Caitlin's Guardian Angel IM #661

The Cutlers of the Shady Lady Ranch
(Yours Truly titles)
Fiona and the Sexy Stranger
Cowboys Are for Loving
Will and the Headstrong Female
The Law and Ginny Marlow
A Match for Morgan
A Triple Threat to Bachelorhood SR #1564

***McClellans & Marinos**
Man Trouble SR #815
The Taming of the Teen SR #839
Babies on His Mind SR #920
The Baby Beneath the Mistletoe SR #1408

***The Alaskans**
Wife in the Mail SE #1217
Stand-In Mom SE #1294
Found: His Perfect Wife SE #1310
The M.D. Meets His Match SE #1401
Lily and the Lawman SE #1467
The Bride Wore Blue Jeans SE #1565

***The Pendletons**
Baby in the Middle SE #892
Husband: Some Assembly Required SE #931

The Mom Squad
A Billionaire and a Baby SE #1528
A Bachelor and a Baby SD #1503
The Baby Mission IM #1220
Beauty and the Baby IM #1668

Cavanaugh Justice
Racing Against Time IM #1249
Crime and Passion IM #1256
Internal Affair Silhouette Books
Dangerous Games IM #1274
The Strong Silent Type SE #1613
Cavanaugh's Woman SE #1617

*Unflashed series

MARIE FERRARELLA

This RITA® Award-winning author has written over one hundred and twenty books for Silhouette, some under the name Marie Nicole. Her romances are beloved by fans worldwide.

MEET THE CAVANAUGHS...

Detective **Shaw Cavanaugh** loves a good movie but when it comes to real life, there's no room for actors. So when Moira decides to use him as research for her next film, he's none too pleased. But then Shaw learns the hard way she's more than a pretty face—she may just be the woman of his dreams!

Movie star **Moira McCormick** wants to shadow someone who won't be starstruck and Shaw shows all evidence of fitting the bill. She likes his indifference to her and wonders if he's hiding what she's hiding—a lethal attraction.

Former police chief **Andrew Cavanaugh** loves his children and hides from them his secret quest to find his long-lost love. Fifteen years ago his wife disappeared and Andrew won't give up hope that she'll come home....

Rose "Claire" Cavanaugh went out for a drive fifteen years ago and found herself with a new identity and no recollection of her past. Can a kindly, handsome man who claims to be her husband bring her back to the fold?

* * *

Let's not forget other members of the Cavanaugh brood:
Callie (*Racing Against Time,* IM#1249),
Clay (*Crime and Passion,* IM#1256),
Patrick (*Internal Affair,* Silhouette Books),
Rayne (*Dangerous Games,* IM#1274)
and Teri (*The Strong Silent Type,* IM#1613).

Chapter One

The sound of the back door closing resounded through the morning air. The last of his offspring had gone off to work. Rising from the table, Andrew Cavanaugh struggled against the wall of loneliness that threatened to close on him.

Last night had been a surprise. He'd come home from the movies only to have Teri tell him that she was getting married. To her partner on the force—one Detective Jack Hawkins.

Of course, he had to admit that he'd seen it coming. Seen the way the young man had gazed at his middle daughter when he thought no one else was looking.

Probably just the same way he had looked at his Rose once. Right up until the day she'd vanished from his life more than fifteen years ago.

Andrew sighed as he gathered up the last of the breakfast dishes from the table. The others had already left to begin their day on the Aurora police force. The way he once had, before he retired.

Retirement was highly overrated.

Maybe he should start thinking about taking on consulting jobs, Andrew mused. At least that would keep him busy.

That made four now, he thought, stacking the dishes on the counter beside the sink. Four out of his five children were getting married soon, not to mention that Patrick, one of his four nephews, had suddenly decided to settle down, as well. All out of the blue, just like that. One minute they were too busy to draw two breaths together, much less get serious about someone; the next, they were making plans, making commitments. Moving on with their lives to the next level.

About time. He was thrilled for them.

Andrew paused, looking around the cheery kitchen. With the silence, he thought of how empty the house was going to seem soon.

It made him miss Rose all the more.

Maybe he should go back up there, he decided, to that little diner his youngest, daughter, Rayne, had discovered while working on one of her cases. The same diner where Rose had surfaced after all these years.

Except that it wasn't Rose, at least not in her mind. The woman he had gone to see, to reclaim, didn't remember who she was, didn't remember the family they'd created. She'd stared at him blankly when he'd turned up at her garden apartment, armed with a book of photographs and the knowledge that she really was his long-lost wife. He covertly got a sample of her fingerprints and had them run against the ones found on her favorite book. That had given him that final tangible proof. She could wear any name tag she wanted pinned to the front of her pink-and-white uniform, call herself anything she pleased, but she was still his Rose.

As gently as he could, he'd tried to convince her of that. It frustrated him that all he'd managed to do was make her sunny smile disappear. She'd withdrawn into herself right before his eyes and become upset. So, while everything within him had begged him to stay until he could convince her she was who he said she was, Andrew had retreated. He'd left the mother of his children with the novel, a copy of *Gone with the Wind,* and his phone number in case things began coming back to her.

He'd hoped that she would have called him by now, but she hadn't. Maybe if he went, tried to persuade her a little, that might do the trick....

Something caught his attention. Andrew stopped and cocked his head.

Was that the doorbell?

Telling himself he was probably hearing things, he nonetheless stopped rinsing the dishes before stacking them in the dishwasher and shut off the tap water. He walked a little closer to the front of the house.

The soft peal of the doorbell again disturbed the atmosphere. He grabbed a towel and dried his hands as he made his way to the front door. Slinging the towel over his right shoulder, Andrew reached for the doorknob and swung the door open. "What did you forget?"

The words hung in the air, mocking him, as he looked into the face of the woman who called herself Claire—the woman his heart knew was Rose.

The soft-spoken blonde on his doorstep looked nervous, vulnerable and more than a little wary. It took her a moment before she responded.

"Everything, apparently."

It took Andrew longer to recover. He'd lived the last fifteen years imagining this very scenario from every possible angle. He'd envisioned Rose tired, jubilant, even contrite, but he'd never once thought there would be a vacant, confused look in her eyes.

He heard himself whisper the words in grateful awe. "You came."

"I had to," she confessed. When he went to take her arm to usher her in, Claire shrank back a little, then offered him a rueful look as she walked into the house unassisted. She hadn't meant to flinch.

Reflexes were responsible for that, reflexes that had been there when she'd woken up, not knowing who or where she was. "I had to see if there was some truth to this story you told me. If I really was this Rose Gallagher Cavanaugh you said I was."

Even as she said the name, it meant nothing to her, created no spark, shed no light. Evoked no feeling of a connection, however distant, existing between her and this woman she was supposed to have been.

But there was something about this man's eyes, something about the way he looked at her, that stirred a faraway, vague feeling, like a breeze blowing along a feather, moving it, but letting it remain where it was.

She wanted—no, *needed*—the feather to become airborne. She was tired of not knowing. Tired of being afraid.

"Not was," Andrew corrected gently. "Are."

Claire nodded, though not in agreement. She nodded in acknowledgment of his words. A sigh escaped her lips before she could stop it. For just the slightest moment, her guard was down.

"I'm so tired of not knowing."

Andrew's mind began to race, making plans. "Can you stay the day?"

He didn't dare hope for more. But even in that short amount of time, he could gather the clan together. Maybe seeing them in person, hearing their voices, might jar something loose for her, might make her start to remember. He knew nothing about amnesia except for what he'd read on the subject in the past few days. This was all virgin territory for him, but he meant to conquer it. Meant to have his Rose back in mind, not just in body.

"I can stay longer than that."

Claire looked around slowly, taking in everything, searching for a memory that wasn't there. From what she could see, it was a comfortable house, warm, inviting, so much larger than what she was accustomed to.

But there was no feeling of homecoming, no subtle suggestion to her subconscious that this was the journey's end. That her questions were finally going to have answers she could accept.

Nothing.

She looked at him again, this man with his blue-gray, hopeful eyes. "I told Lucy I'm taking that vacation I was always putting off," she said, referring to the woman who was both her boss and her best friend, the woman who had given her shelter when she'd wandered in off the road, frightened and lost, all those years ago. "She told me to take as long as I liked, seeing as how I had over two months coming to me."

Two months. He had two months, Andrew thought. That should be enough time to make her remember. He'd make it be enough time.

"You can stay in Callie's old room," he told her, pointing out the way.

Claire merely nodded and followed him.

* * *

''You have any idea what this is about?'' Detective Shaw Cavanaugh asked his partner Detective Steven Reese as they walked to the office of the chief of detectives.

A half head shorter than his partner, Reese ran a hand along the two-day-old stubble on his chin. It never ceased to amaze Shaw that Reese *always* seemed to be sporting two days' worth of stubble—no more, no less. Reese claimed it was sexy. Shaw saw it as an excuse not to shave on a regular basis.

Reese's broad shoulders rose and fell beneath a jacket that was a tad less than fashionable. ''Hey, Chief Cavanaugh's your uncle, not mine.''

Shaw shook his head. If this was remotely personal, Uncle Brian would have called him up at home, or even dropped by his apartment. In his family, they all enjoyed that kind of an easy relationship with one another, feeling free to pop up on each other's doorstep whenever the need arose. This was something different, something work related.

''I don't think his being my uncle has anything to do with this.''

At the precinct, personal family structure was forgotten. They were all brothers and sisters under the uniform. The fact that nine of them, not counting the chief, were related by blood just made them a shade closer, that was all. But at the moment, their closeness didn't help shed any light for Shaw on what was going on.

"Maybe the chief is going to ask how come you haven't succumbed to Cupid's arrows like the rest of your family." Reese smirked. "And he's invited me along to throw your suspicions off."

Shaw rolled his eyes even though he knew that scenario wasn't even remotely possible. "Shut up. I get enough of that from my father."

It was all well-meaning, Shaw knew. His father worried about him. Worried that while Callie, Teri and Rayne, not to mention Clay, had all found their soul mates, Shaw's own love life had been on the low-key.

So low-key that at times it didn't even register a pulse. But then, he'd always been the serious one in his family. He didn't believe in partying, or in wasting someone's time if he had no intentions of becoming serious with that person. And he had no intentions of ever getting serious because being a policeman meant maintaining a tenuous partnership with death. It rode in your squad car with you every day and could claim you at any time, without warning. Coming to terms with one's mortality was hard enough; asking someone else to accept it was out of the question. He didn't want a wife to make that sacrifice with him.

His uncle Mike had died while on the job and he'd seen his best friend killed in the line of duty. To make matters worse, his best friend had been engaged to his sister Callie at the time a bullet had cut him down. Shaw had watched, unable to help his sister work her way through the almost paralyzing heartache and grief that followed.

Shaw had sworn never to put anyone he cared about in a position to grieve over him. The only way to avoid this was by not getting involved in the first place. As far as he was concerned, he was doing fine. He just had to convince everyone else of that.

Shaw looked at his partner sharply, replaying part of the man's last words. Reese talked as if he knew that his brother and sisters were committed to marching down the aisle and plighting their everlasting love. At last count, Teri hadn't been among that group. That was this morning's news.

His eyes narrowed to two bright blue slits. ''How did you know?'' They'd been partners for three years and in that time, Shaw felt as if Reese had learned to read him better than most husbands could read their wives. But this went beyond the norm.

''About Teri?'' Reese offered him a gleaming white, toothy grin. ''Haven't you heard? Word travels fast around here.'' He shook his head in wonder. ''Gotta admit, though, it was one of the first times I've ever seen Hawk grin. Kinda scary.''

Shaw laughed shortly. ''That's because Teri hasn't cooked for him yet.''

Reese's laugh echoed his partner's. ''Like your father would ever let her get close to the stove. He'll just set another place at the table,'' he predicted. A small note of longing entered his voice. ''You Cavanaughs don't know how lucky you've got it. Only thing my old man knew how to make was TV dinners—and he usually burned them.''

The lament bore no weight with Shaw. ''Hey, you know you've got a standing invitation to the house, day or night. Nothing my dad likes better than feeding a fellow cop.''

Before he'd retired, Andrew Cavanaugh had worked his way up through the ranks to become chief of the entire Aurora Police Department. It was a known fact that he thought of all the officers on the force as members of his extended family. His door was always open and his table was always available.

Reese paused. They were standing right in front of the chief's door. Sobering somewhat, he glanced at his taller, handsomer partner.

''You sure you didn't do anything that would get us called out on the carpet?''

Shaw's eyes met his. There was barely a hint of amusement in them as he said, ''Other than have you for a partner, no.''

Never one to hesitate, Shaw knocked on the door once, then opened it. He didn't bother waiting for an invitation.

Shaw was fortunate that the man wasn't in the middle of talking, or else he might have been in danger of swallowing his tongue.

Or, at the very least, gagging on it.

His uncle Brian was not alone.

Rather than sitting at his desk, surrounded by piles of papers, Brian Cavanaugh, considered more than passingly handsome and a great deal younger-looking than his fifty years of age, stood on the far side of his desk, talking to a striking-looking blonde, who sat opposite him.

Even as Shaw took in the scene, the blonde turned and looked directly at him with the greenest pair of eyes he'd ever seen.

The second before he collected himself, Shaw felt as if a four-hundred-pound linebacker had just jumped on his chest before grabbing the game-winning football away from him.

The woman wore a light blue, two-piece suit. Powder-blue, he thought it was called by people, such as his sisters, who had more than six colors within their mental repertoire. Whatever the color was called, it appeared that most of the material had been used up making the jacket because there was precious little left over for the skirt.

Not that he would have registered a complaint with anyone. The less skirt there was, the more leg was visible. And he had to admit that the woman had the longest, shapeliest legs he'd ever seen.

Belatedly, Shaw realized that his saliva had completely disappeared. Which made up for the fact, he supposed, that Reese stood beside him, almost visibly drooling.

A vague feeling buzzed around in his slightly disoriented brain that he recognized the woman from somewhere, although for the life of him, Shaw couldn't have said where. He supposed if it mattered, his uncle would fill him in. If it didn't matter, he didn't need to be wasting time trying to remember.

Like a five-star general who finally saw the key members of his army come into view, Brian Cavanaugh clapped his hands together.

"And here they are now," the chief said, although it was obvious that while he said "they," he was looking at only one of them. He was looking at Shaw.

Shaw nodded a respectful greeting toward his uncle, then let his eyes move back toward the woman.

Was this a personal case his uncle wanted to be handled discreetly?

It didn't seem very likely, but stranger things had turned out to be true. Since he and Reese were assigned to Vice and Narcotics, he wondered just what this woman's connection was to the shady world that he was sometimes required to travel through. The mistress of an up-and-coming drug lord, ready to turn state's evidence in exchange for immunity and a new identity?

Or was there a more personal connection?

He stopped speculating and decided to wait out his uncle, who was smiling wider than ever.

Shaw then became aware that his venerable partner, the man he relied on to guard his back and be the other set of eyes to sharply watch the mean streets, had stopped breathing. Reese had sucked in one long breath and then nothing.

Shaw turned to look at him and saw that Reese's brown eyes were all but riveted to the blonde. Turning his back ever so slightly toward her, Shaw lowered both his head and his voice as he asked, "Reese, you okay?"

All Reese could manage was a slightly wooden nod. His eyes never left the woman's face.

Shaw heard his uncle clear his throat and realized the man was doing it to hide a laugh. Brian was laid-back, but ordinarily all business during working hours.

Just what the hell was going on here?

He noted that the woman looked a little concerned, rather than amused, by the obvious effect she was having on Shaw's partner. Maybe she wasn't as accustomed to men becoming tongue-tied, drooling and breathless around her as he'd thought.

"Would you like some water?"

Her voice was lyrical.

He'd half expected her to have a grating voice. It would have been nature's way of balancing things out. Someone as beautiful as this woman couldn't possibly have the voice of an angel. But she did. An angel who originated from somewhere in the deep South if his ear served him right. There was just the smallest hint of a Georgia lilt to her tone.

Or maybe he was just hallucinating. What the hell had gotten into him today?

When his partner made no response to her question, she pulled her lips back in a quick grin. Shaw had seen lighthouse beacons that possessed less wattage.

And then, as if by some miracle, Reese came back from the dead. "Are you—? Are you—?"

Shaw snorted in abject disgust. His partner, known for his interrogation skills, couldn't even complete a simple four-word sentence.

The green-eyed goddess-on-earth apparently understood his garbled attempt at communication. She smiled again and said, "Yes, I am."

Well, that cleared up nothing, Shaw thought, beginning to get annoyed.

He took police work very seriously. Every moment he was here, watching an episode of *High School Confidential* unfold was a moment he wasn't sending the bad guys to jail.

Just what was it they were doing here? Shifting impatiently, Shaw looked to his uncle for a logical explanation.

"My nephew doesn't get to the movies very much," the chief told her.

What did going to the movies have to do with anything?

And then it hit him.

Shaw suddenly remembered where he'd seen the woman's face before. Not in some covertly taken photograph of a drug lord with his high-priced mistress, but looking down at him from the giant screen of his local movie theater. Callie had dragged him there a little more than a month ago to view some romantic comedy whose name and plot escaped him at the moment.

Beside him Reese had returned from the land of the living zombies and rediscovered his tongue. His partner hit his shoulder with the back of his hand, as if that would make him return to his senses.

As if he'd been the one to leave them, Shaw thought, regain control over himself. She was a woman, a mortal woman, even if she did look like a goddess.

"Don't you know who this is, Cavanaugh?" Reese demanded. "This is Moira McCormick."

And that and two dollars, Shaw thought, singularly unimpressed, would get him a ride on the bus.

Chapter Two

He wasn't impressed by her.

Good, Moira thought.

She didn't want him to be impressed. While the reaction of the man standing next to the chief of detectives' nephew was sweet and more than a little flattering, ultimately it would only get in the way of what she wanted. She needed to get inside her character, and to do that, she needed a clear, unobstructed view of what life was like for a member of the vice squad. Moira McCormick believed in doing her homework and this was homework. Homework was never effectively dealt with when you were busy having a good time.

She'd spent a good deal of her life focusing on becoming exactly what she was, a highly regarded film star who was, thankfully, in great demand. That wasn't something that had come easily. She certainly hadn't arrived at her present position in life by sitting around, allowing others to fawn on her while she lapped up well-meaning but, for the most part, empty compliments.

Making her dream a reality took work. She worked hard to make it all look easy, effortless. And she had a feeling that it was going to take a lot of effort to make this unsmiling detective with the piercing blue eyes come around to her side of the table.

"You haven't heard of me," she concluded.

"I've heard of you." In the last seven years, he'd seen maybe five movies. He believed in other forms of diversion. If he needed to knock off some steam, he turned to sports. He loved basketball and baseball the most, but almost any sport, other than golf, would do. To him, playing golf seemed too much like standing on the sidelines. Maybe that was why movies seemed such a waste of time to him. Plunking down money for a two-hour vicarious experience had never really sat right with him.

But he knew who she was. He would have had to be living in a cave not to.

Still, if she was expecting him to turn into a puddle of pulsating semisolid flesh, the way Reese apparently had, she was in for a disappointment.

Moira nodded. The detective's reply had an air of finality to it. Which meant he wasn't going to gush.

Which meant he was perfect.

She still had doubts about his partner, though, but that could be handled. Worst-case scenario, she could get Chief Cavanaugh to reassign the shorter detective to another partner for the time being.

She wanted the stubborn one. In her gut, she knew he'd be the one to show her the ropes, the one who wouldn't sugarcoat things. She wouldn't take no for an answer.

Flashing another brilliant smile, Moira turned toward the chief of detectives. ''You're right. He's perfect.''

Shaw didn't like the sound of this. Wary, feeling like someone who'd just been blindfolded and pushed out onto a very thin tightrope, he looked from the movie star to his uncle.

''Perfect for what? What's going on here, Chief?'' For the first time he saw that the woman had a small, thick spiral notebook on the desk in front of her. She was making notations in it. ''Why's she doing that?''

''Ms. McCormick is about to make a movie dealing with an inner-city vice squad,'' Brian said cautiously.

''Good for her,'' Shaw bit off.

His uncle looked at him sharply and Shaw inclined his head by way of a minor apology. It was just that he didn't see the point of making movies about the kinds of thing he and Reese dealt with on a daily basis. At best, his work could be described as long spates of monotony interrupted by pockets of adrenaline-rushing moments comprised of sheer danger and terror. If portrayed accurately, no one would come to see the movie because the kind of life they led was boring ninety-seven percent of the time. If not portrayed accurately, why bother making the movie at all? In his experience, movies such as the one his uncle was describing were just excuses to blow up a lot of things.

He had no use for that kind of so-called entertainment.

Shaw turned his attention back to the woman who was watching him so intently. Was she expecting him to perform tricks? He wasn't about to be anyone's trained monkey or stooge.

"You know, I'm a huge fan," his partner was saying, taking Moira's small hand in his and shaking it again. "I've seen all your movies."

Very carefully, she managed to extricate her hand without giving offense. That, too, was training from way back when.

"So you're the one." She laughed.

Reese looked at her, his face a mask of confusion. Moira McCormick's movies broke records. There was even talk of there being an Oscar nomination for her last role as a turn-of-the-century Irish freedom fighter. How could she downplay attendance?

"What? Oh, that's a joke?" And then Reese

laughed as if he'd just caught the humor of it. He looked up at her much like a puppy looked at its master.

Shaw struggled not to scowl. He'd never seen Reese like this. Just showed you never really knew a person. His impatience began to break through.

"So you want to do what? Ask us questions? Pick our brains?" He glanced at his partner. "Such as they are," he added.

Moira exchanged looks with the chief. It was clear that she wanted to take the lead here. "Actually, I'd like to do more than that."

He *really* didn't like the sound of this. He especially didn't like the fact that his uncle had obviously yielded center stage to this Hollywood bit of fluff.

"More?" he echoed. "More as in how?"

"As in riding along with you for the next week or so." She uttered every word as if it were a sane request.

If granted at all, ride-alongs were usually conducted by patrol officers along routes they knew ahead of time were going to be safe, or as safe as could be hoped for. He and Reese did not patrol fantasyland. They went where the action was.

This time, he scowled darkly at her. "During work hours?"

Moira had a feeling she was being challenged. Nothing made her feel more alive. It reminded her of the old days. "That would be the point."

"Oh, no, no. Sorry, out of the question. We don't do taxi service."

Brian took a step forward, his message clear. Shaw was to toe the line.

"Shaw—" Brian began, then looked surprised as Moira held up her hand, unconsciously silencing him. Ever since she could remember, she was accustomed to fighting every battle for herself. She'd come here looking for resistance, because only a real, dedicated detective was going to be of use to her.

"You wouldn't be driving me around. I'd be an observer. You wouldn't even know I was there," Moira assured him.

The way she looked at him made Shaw feel as if there was no one else in the room. He supposed that was part of her attraction. And her weapon. He shook himself mentally free.

"I highly doubt that."

A man would have to be dead three days to be oblivious to her. He saw amusement play along her lips. Shaw deliberately shifted his eyes toward his uncle, who seemed rather amused by the whole exchange. Had everyone gone crazy? Shaw shifted, his body language asking for a private audience with his uncle.

"With all due respect, sir, wouldn't she be better off observing another woman?" He thought of his sister. Now there was someone who wouldn't mind serving as tour guide. She had the patience, the temperament for it. "Callie, for instance—"

Brian shook his head. "None of the female detectives are in Vice and Vice is what Ms. McCormick wants to observe."

"Then team her up with another pair of detectives," he suggested firmly.

Reese made a strange, protesting noise that sounded like the gurgle of a castaway going down for the third time.

Moira hardly heard the other man. Her attention was focused on Shaw. It was this man or no one.

"I don't want another pair of detectives," she told him, rising to her feet and looking up into his eyes. She wasn't a short woman, but he made her feel like one. Was he protesting because this arrangement would make his girlfriend jealous? "I want this pair."

"No offense, ma'am," he said evenly, "but what you want really doesn't concern me."

Ma'am, she thought. If she tried hard, she could almost see him tipping the brim of an off-white Stetson. Because this man was off-white, not the pure hero type, not quite the black-hearted loner he made himself out to be.

It's going to be fun, getting under your skin, Detective Cavanaugh, she thought. And fun was part of the reason she was in this business. The money was the other, because without money, she wouldn't be able to take care of those who needed caring for.

"It does this time, Detective," Brian told his nephew sternly. "Ms. McCormick requested a detective who wasn't going to get bowled over by the fact that she earns her living making films." He looked at Reese. "I'm assuming that you'll be able to pull yourself together and do the department proud by tomorrow."

"Tomorrow?" Moira repeated. She was clearly disappointed. At least that was something, Shaw thought. "I was hoping we could get started today."

Brian shook his head. He hadn't gotten to where he was by being unreasonable. "I think Detective Cavanaugh would appreciate a day's head start to prepare for this 'role' himself. Wouldn't you, Detective?"

"At least," Shaw muttered. That gave him a little less than twenty-four hours to come up with an excuse, he thought.

Moira had learned long ago to take disappointment well. It was in her nature to roll with any punch that was thrown. A nomadic life with a con-artist father who was always one step in front of the law had taught her that.

She nodded, glancing at her perfect candidate's partner. She knew if it was up to Detective Reese, they would get started this moment. But Detective Cavanaugh was the one who piqued her interest.

"Fine. Bright and early tomorrow morning, then?" she asked Shaw.

"Bright and early," Shaw responded. The words squeezed themselves out through teeth that were tightly clenched.

Damn it. Why him? Why, of all the available candidates in the precinct, had he been the one to have gotten the short straw? He hadn't even picked it, it had been thrust into his hand. Any one of the others would have been happy about having this motivation-seeking pain-in-the-butt riding around with them. His uncle had only to look around to know that.

For the remainder of the day, from what Shaw could see, Moira McCormick stayed at the precinct, initially getting a grand tour from his uncle, then being handed off to another beaming detective, Ed Rafferty. The latter, usually the personification of grumpiness, was beaming from ear to ear as he took her from one department to the other. Ordinarily, Rafferty spent his time behind a desk since a bullet had found him one dreary twilight, giving him a permanent limp and an overwhelming desire to remain among the living.

From the sound of it, Moira McCormick had an unending supply of questions. Great. Just what he needed, Shaw thought miserably.

Shaw steered clear of the traveling circus with its growing audience. For most of the day, he wasn't even in the precinct. A snitch known to him only as Barlow had called offering up for sale a tiny piece of the current puzzle he and Reese were pondering.

Shaw had bought the information from him, telling Barlow to secure more. He and Reese were following up on what had started out as a simple prostitution bust and was turning out to be a rather intricate sex-for-hire ring that dealt with underage prostitutes.

There were days when the good guys won and days when the bad guys did. This, Shaw thought, stretching out his legs before him as he sank into his chair, was one for the bad guys.

Maybe it would be better tomorrow.

And then he remembered. Tomorrow Miss Hollywood would be in his car. Tomorrow would definitely *not* be better. The only thing he could hope for was that she would quickly tire of playing the role of researcher. He'd given one more try at talking his way into a reprieve, but his uncle wasn't about to grant it.

"Look, it's for the good of the city," Brian had said. "They're going to be filming a lot of the outdoor shots here. That's going to bring in a great deal of money, Shaw. Money's good for the local economy, good for the force. Salaries don't come from the tooth fairy."

The discussion, Shaw knew, had been doomed from the get-go.

Contemplating tomorrow, his mood hadn't been the best. It got decidedly worse in the afternoon when he'd walked into the precinct and saw her standing in the middle of a wide circle of his fellow officers. She signed autographs and behaved like a benevolent queen bestowing favors on her subjects.

As he'd gone toward his cubicle, Moira McCormick had turned her head in his direction and their eyes had met over the heads of the officers around her. She smiled at him, directly at him, and something had stirred inside his gut.

Probably the chili he'd grabbed for lunch.

He had to get something better than lunch wagon fare, Shaw told himself as he'd sunk into his chair.

Reese, he noted, stayed behind with the throng around Moira.

There *had* to be a way to get out of this.

But even as he thought about it, Shaw knew it wasn't possible. Once his uncle made up his mind, that was it. Brian Cavanaugh didn't say things just to hear himself talk. And there was the matter of the extra revenue to the city coffers. Times were tough. No one was going to turn his back on money.

A week. It would be over in a week. He had to keep telling himself that.

"Hey, Shaw, I just heard about your new assignment."

He didn't have to look up to know that the gleeful voice belonged to his brother. Clay dropped into the chair beside his desk, grinning broadly.

"Always said that Uncle Brian liked you best." Clay glanced over his shoulder toward the movie star and the ever-increasing crowd around her. "Just never thought you'd hit the jackpot like this."

He didn't bother asking where Clay had gotten his information about the ride-along. Rumors flew around the precinct faster than a hummingbird gathering breakfast and there had been over eight hours for the news to get out. If he didn't miss his guess, it had probably been all over the precinct within the first ten minutes.

"No jackpot," he told Clay evenly. "It's just a damn annoying baby-sitting assignment."

"Some baby." Clay hooted with the proper amount of appreciation. "Moira McCormick can play at being my baby anytime."

Before Clay had settled down and lost his heart to Ilene, he'd been involved with more women than could be found in the population of any given Alaskan town. Now that he thought of it, this kind of assignment was definitely more up his brother's alley than his, Shaw decided, but he knew there was no use in suggesting it to his uncle.

Picking up a paper clip from a caddy on his desk, Shaw began to straighten it out. "I'm sure Ilene will be thrilled to hear that."

At the mention of his fiancée's name, Clay sobered ever so slightly. Shaw knew that there was no way his brother would jeopardize what he had for something as insignificant as a fling with a movie star, or anyone else, no matter how tempting—and this woman gave the word *temptation* a whole new, deeper meaning. However, Clay's wild-oat-sowing days were now behind him.

Unlike him, Shaw thought. Wild-oat sowing had never been in his makeup. He vaguely wondered if he was missing something, then dismissed the thought.

"Hey," Clay protested, "don't get me wrong—"

Shaw laughed, tossing aside the wavy paper clip. "Easy, stop sweating. I'm not going to tell Ilene you became a drooling moron like Reese, at least not until there's something in it for me."

He flashed his brother a grin, then looked over toward where Moira was still holding court. The crowd around her just kept getting larger and nosier. He knew that some of the men had called their wives, who promptly put in an appearance. So far, Moira was taking it all with good grace, but then, wasn't that what movie stars liked? Adulation?

Shaw blew out a breath. "Look, what's the big deal? So she's beautiful, so what? Beauty is only skin deep. Take that away and what do you have?"

Clay looked over his shoulder again and sighed. When he looked back at Shaw, there was a slightly lopsided smile curving his lips. "A damn sexy skeleton, I'm willing to bet."

"Any way you can ask Brian for this assignment?"

Clay vehemently shook his head. "Oh, no, that's all I need—to tell Ilene I'm going to be riding around in my car with Moira McCormick at my elbow."

He thought of his brother's fiancée. "Why should that be a problem? Ilene's a gorgeous woman."

"No argument, but she's not a movie star."

Shaw laughed shortly, picking up another paper clip and going to work on it. "Thank God."

"You know what I mean." The sound of Moira's laughter floated back to them, somehow managing to rise above the din. Shaw's frown only deepened as Clay said, "There's an aura around them."

"They're people, same as you and me. Two hands, two feet, one head, a torso in between. Same parts."

"But they look better."

If he didn't know better, he would have said that Clay was smitten with the paper person at the other end of the room.

"That's lighting, nothing more. And without it, they fall apart. Actors tend to be illusions. You want to know why the good ones are so good at what they do, why they can take on other roles so easily?" Warming to his subject, Shaw leaned forward. "Because they have no substance of their own, nothing to rework. They're shape-shifters, Clay, as interesting as the parts they play—nothing more." He paused. A strange look flashed across Clay's face, half amusement, half unease. "What's the matter with you? You look as if you've seen a ghost."

And then he felt a hand on his shoulder and knew the reason for Clay's odd expression before he ever heard her say a thing. ''Not a ghost. A shape-shifter, I think you called me.''

Shaw slowly turned his chair around. Moira McCormick was standing behind his desk. The entourage that had been hovering around her had melted into the background, watching the exchange like an audience in search of entertainment.

By the looks on their faces, he'd delivered, big-time.

''I was talking in general terms,'' Shaw said.

''I think it was an apt description,'' she replied cheerfully. ''Shape-shifter.'' Moira rolled the word on her tongue, as if testing how it felt. ''I like it.'' She lowered her voice as she nodded toward the others behind her. ''And I like the fact that you didn't join in back there.''

''I'm not a joiner.''

''I sensed that.'' She made herself comfortable on the edge of his desk. ''A rebel, right?''

''No, just an average Joe, out to earn a living.''

''That's not what your uncle said.'' Brian Cavanaugh had nothing but glowing words for the man he'd coupled her with. There were a number of good things to be said about Steven Reese, as well, but to an extent, the latter had negated it with his clear case of adoration.

''The chief says a lot of things.'' Shaw rose, taking care not to brush against her as he did. For once, he was going home early. He couldn't get anything done here, not with these hyenas hovering about, ready to burst out laughing. ''Good night.''

''Good night.'' As she watched him leave, she couldn't help thinking that the man she'd selected had a very nice posterior. She was going to enjoy watching him walk away. ''I'll see you in the morning.''

Shaw said nothing. It was a prophecy he really wished he could avert.

As he left the room, he heard Moira saying something to his brother. Clay began to laugh in response.

It was going to be a long week.

Chapter Three

If he had any intention of dwelling on the scene he'd just left, or on the woman who was going to be disrupting his life for the next week, Shaw found he had no time. His cell phone was ringing before he reached his car in the lot.

Digging it out of his pocket, he flipped open the lid. "Cavanaugh."

"Shaw, I need you to come home."

Twilight began to whisper along the fringes of the tree-lined parking lot. Shaw stopped walking, stopped thinking about how much Moira McCormick was going to impede his current investigation. His father was on the other end of the call and there was definitely something wrong. His father rarely, if ever, called during working hours.

Shaw couldn't begin to fathom his tone. He could usually read his father like a well-loved book. Concern nudged at the edges of his mind. "Dad, is there something wrong?"

There was a pause, but no explanation followed. "Just come home. Now."

Shaw didn't waste time asking any more questions. He knew his father wasn't given to drama. Whatever was going on, it was important.

"I'll be right there," he promised. Shutting his cell, Shaw was in his car and on the open road in less time than it took to think through the process.

He wouldn't allow his mind to explore possibilities. The closest his father had ever come to sounding so urgent was when Uncle Mike had been fatally shot.

But no one at the precinct had said anything. If there was an officer down, much less a member of his own family, word would have gotten to him by now. Uncle Brian would have called him into his office immediately.

The more Shaw thought, the more he realized that the only other time his father had sounded so somber was when he'd gathered the family together to tell them that their mother's car had been found at the bottom of the river. His father had gone on to say that there was every hope in the world that she had somehow managed to survive the accident.

That was his father, an optimist to the end even though he wasn't usually vocal about it.

Even as the years went by and no clue of Rose Cavanaugh's survival came to light, his father had never, ever given up hope that someday she would come walking through the front door to take back her place in their lives.

Waiting at a stoplight, Shaw scrubbed his hand over his face. Hell of a man, his father. Shaw didn't know how he would have handled losing his wife that way and being left to raise five kids to boot. Shaw smiled to himself. He had to hand it to the old man—they didn't make 'em like that anymore.

He wondered if Andrew Cavanaugh knew that he was his kids' hero. Probably not.

As he approached his father's house, Shaw saw that other cars were ahead of him. A quick scan told him that Callie, Rayne and Teri had gotten there ahead of him. One glance in his rearview mirror indicated Clay's vehicle was right behind him.

Ordinarily, that wouldn't have disturbed him. His father used any excuse to get them all together beyond the call to breakfast that he issued every day. Like as not, most mornings would find him making a pit stop at the family house, not so much for the food, which was always good, as for the company. Granted, he and his siblings all went their separate ways—his father encouraged that. But something always pulled them together no matter how independent they were.

His father had taught them that roots were by far the most important things in life. If you had deep enough roots, you could withstand any kind of storm that came your way.

Shaw couldn't help wondering if there was a storm coming, or if it had already arrived.

After parking beside the mailbox, just behind Callie's vehicle, Shaw got out of his car just as Clay pulled up behind him.

His brother was quick to climb out, slamming the door in his wake. One look at his brother's face told him that Clay was as puzzled as he was for this sudden summons to return home.

"You have any idea what this is all about?" Clay asked.

Shaw shook his head. "Only that Dad said to come home."

"Not like him to be so dramatic," Clay speculated, frowning and falling into place beside him.

Because he was the oldest and the others looked to him to set the tone, Shaw remained deliberately low-keyed. "Maybe Teri's changed her mind about Hawk," he deadpanned, then nodded toward the door. "Only one way to find out."

Neither one of them bothered to knock. They all had their keys, something their father insisted on. This had been their first home and it would remain their home no matter how far away they went. For Andrew, it was as simple as that.

"Okay, Dad, what's the big mystery?" Clay called out, following Shaw into the living room.

Clay stopped dead right behind his brother.

His sisters were already in the room along with their father. They all sat on the sofa, smiling but looking far more subdued than Shaw ever remembered seeing them. The reason was seated rigidly on the recliner their father favored.

A ghost from the past.

The polite but strained conversation stopped the moment he and Clay entered the room.

For a single second, Shaw's heart stopped beating as he was thrown back in time, then pushed forward to the present again. Hardly daring to breathe, he looked from the woman to his father, who nodded.

He wasn't a police detective anymore, he was a son. A son whose missing mother had turned up in his living room.

They were already aware that Rose Cavanaugh was alive. His father had told them of Rayne's discovery, of going up and seeing for himself the woman who answered to the name of Claire. He had wanted to persuade her to come home with him. Shaw also knew that the woman claimed not to have any memory of them.

Shaw could see a great deal of unresolved emotion in his father's eyes. He could also see that while she was looking straight ahead at them, trying to smile, the woman who didn't appear to know she was his mother was digging her fingertips into the leather armrests.

"And these are your sons, Shaw and Clay," Andrew told her.

The woman inclined her head, rising slightly from her seat, and succeeded in smiling at them. At him. Smiling at him with his mother's smile.

Shaw had no idea what to feel, what to think.

And then she shook her head, sorrow in her eyes as she turned them toward his father. Her apology throbbed with emotion, with unshed tears. "I'm sorry, I don't remember them, either."

Andrew nodded, resigned but ever hopeful. "You will," he promised. "It'll take time but you will." He didn't have a single strain of doubt in his voice. Andrew looked at his sons. There was triumph in his expression. "Boys, Claire has agreed to stay here with us for a while."

Shaw raised his eyes toward his father, waiting for an explanation. Questions began to form in his mind.

"Claire?" he echoed.

"It's my name," the woman told him quietly. "At least, that's the only name I've known for the past fifteen years."

Her voice was soft, like his mother's voice. Shaw felt an ache take hold. There was nothing he could do to fix this except ride it out. Compassion welled up within him. He sincerely felt for his father.

Unable to hold back any longer, Rayne was on

her feet, standing in front of Claire. "That's because you disappeared fifteen years ago," she insisted. "You *are* our mother, you *are* his wife. Why can't you see that?"

Her voice broke even as Shaw crossed to her. Ever protective of his siblings, especially of Rayne, who'd always been the most troubled and the most tormented by all this, he put his arm around his sister.

"This is why we never let you become a psychiatrist," he teased, trying to lighten the moment if only a fraction. He kissed the top of her head, then he gave her a quick, heartfelt squeeze. Rayne had been the one the most vocal in her suffering when her mother had disappeared after the accident. The youngest, she'd been the most attached. "It's going to be all right, Rayne," Shaw promised. He looked at his mother. "It's just going to take time, but we'll all be there for you. For each other."

Claire seemed filled with remorse that she didn't know them. "I'm so sorry I can't—"

On his feet, Andrew cut her short. "That's okay. Rome wasn't built in a day."

"Now here's something you should remember." Taking her cue from the others, Teri tried to keep the conversation on a light, upbeat path. "Dad always has a corny saying to reinforce his points."

Claire smiled bravely at these strangers around her. She'd been alone for so long, both physically and mentally. Alone, yet haunted by memories that refused to form beyond specters. To believe that there was a family waiting for her, ready to accept her with open arms, was more like a fantasy than reality.

But even so, she couldn't make the wall keeping her from her past come down, couldn't even chip away at it until there was the slightest clink in the mortar. Couldn't access anything beyond the time she regained consciousness, found herself dripping wet and walking along a highway.

Going from nowhere to nowhere.

Andrew looked at the faces of his children. "Okay." He clapped his hands together. "Let's eat."

Shaw laughed and shook his head. Food was his father's solution to almost any dilemma. He maintained that if you had a pleasantly full stomach, problems didn't loom as large.

Shaw had a feeling they were going to have to consume a mountain of food before this was all finally resolved to their satisfaction.

The alarm went off.

Reluctantly, Shaw rolled over on his side and stared at the blue digital numbers. It was early.

He'd always been an early riser. This morning, however, he entertained the idea of succumbing to the unfamiliar desire to remain in bed a little longer. He wanted sleep to anesthetize him.

Didn't matter what he wanted. It didn't work that

way for him; it never had. Once he was awake, he was awake. And the next moment, like marauding soldiers, thoughts came crowding into his head.

Thoughts of last night with his mother.

It had been one strange evening. He felt as if he'd experienced it on two very different levels, both at the same time. Part of him had wanted to throw his arms around the delicate woman, to tell her how much he'd missed her, to tell her everything that had happened in the past fifteen years. The other part had stood off, afraid of getting hurt. Even so, he'd attempted to get to know this woman who hadn't been a part of their lives for such a long time. She was both their mother and a stranger at the same time.

It was surreal.

So was getting up, knowing that he was going to be riding around with a movie star in the back of his car, he grumbled to himself.

Shaw threw off the covers. The less he thought about that, the better.

What he needed was a cold shower to bring him around. That, and maybe shooting a few hoops at the local park. Getting physical always helped him cope better.

Shaw wondered if Clay was up yet and if he could be persuaded to meet him at the park. Probably not. His brother was a slug. When they were growing up, more than once Clay had offered him money just to grasp five extra minutes in bed. But maybe he could rouse Clay before it was time to get to work.

Looking at the phone, Shaw tried to remember Clay's new number now that he'd moved in with Ilene. He drew a blank.

He'd look for it after his shower, he decided.

A gentle, cool breeze pushed its way into the bedroom. Shaw glanced toward the window, remembering that he'd left it open last night. The breeze stirred the drapes he'd drawn before getting undressed.

Shaw stretched, the muscles of his taut, tanned naked body rippling and moving like an awakening panther.

He decided to leave the window open and walked into his small bathroom.

He had just stepped into the stall when he heard the ringing. At first, he thought it might be his cell phone or his landline, but then he realized that it was the doorbell.

Muttering under his breath, he turned the water off, grabbed a towel to secure around his middle and padded out to the front door. Because there was a threat made against his life—nothing out of the ordinary in his line of work and certainly nothing he was about to share with any of the members of his family—Shaw paused to pick up his second weapon. He took the safety off before approaching the front door.

The towel slid a little and he secured it again before turning his attention back to his unexpected, uninvited guest.

"Who is it?"

"Your shadow." The woman's voice on the other side of the door was flippant.

Shaw lowered his gun. He didn't need any more identification than that. Half expecting one of his siblings to turn up on his doorstep after what had gone down last night, he still knew it wasn't one of his sisters who was standing there now. It was *her*.

Biting off a curse, he yanked open the door and glared at Moira McCormick. God, but he hated being right sometimes.

"What the hell are you doing here?"

Swallowing my tongue at the moment, she thought.

Wow.

It was the only word that even began to cover what her eyes took in. *Magnificent* was a close second.

The jacket Cavanaugh had worn yesterday had given her the impression of wide shoulders, but like as not, coming from the land of illusion the way she did, she knew the silhouette could have been just as much a credit to the tailor who had fashioned the article of clothing as it could have been to time spent in the gym, working out.

Seeing drops of water gleaming on his smooth, muscular chest and more droplets sliding invitingly down to the towel he had haphazardly draped around his waist—a towel that looked as if it were ready to break away at the very next large breath he took in—Moira was hard-pressed to come up with a time when she'd seen a better specimen of manhood.

"Absorbing you," she finally murmured in response to the question he'd snapped at her.

She looked incredibly casual, he thought. Gone were the four-inch heels and the miniskirt, along with the carefully styled hair. She wore jeans, a baggy shirt that still wasn't baggy enough to hide the fact that the lady was well endowed, and on her feet she had on a pair of comfortable sneakers. Her hair was needle straight and loose about her shoulders, a wayward blond cloud.

Looking at her made his body tighten, as if he were on the alert to spring into action at any second. With effort, he exercised as much control over himself as he was able.

"What?" he asked, confused.

Moira tossed her hair back over her shoulder and cleared her throat before she laughed.

"Sorry, I'm not used to having almost naked men opening the door for me." She tried to force her mind onto other things and found that it didn't want to leave. "I came because I wanted to be there from the beginning of your day to the end of it."

He blew out a breath as he closed the door behind her. "And that's going to help you how?"

She decided that maybe it would be better if she

observed her surroundings rather than his attributes. The man kept a messy apartment. There were no female touches anywhere. Which meant that he lived alone. That was good. She didn't want to be walking in on a man in a relationship. She had no desire to make waves for Cavanaugh, just pick his brain.

"Subtle nuances," she told him, still looking around, "things to keep in mind—you'd be surprised."

Shaw was already surprised. Nobody had said anything about the woman showing up on his doorstep at the crack of dawn. "Look, I didn't sign on for this."

He didn't bother adding that he hadn't signed on for any of it, that he would have rather spent three weeks undercover in a sewer without benefit of a shower than to have to dance attendance to some gorgeous, overpaid, spoiled Hollywood airhead who was accustomed to having her every whim catered to.

Cavanaugh was still resisting, which was good, but she didn't want it to be a major issue. She needed to get the research under her belt. She'd already sped-read her way through several books on the subject, but nothing took the place of feeling the action firsthand. She wanted this week to be eye-opening for her. Every movie she made, she was determined that it would be better than the last one. This movie was no exception.

Wandering over to the bookcase that stood to the right of his twenty-seven-inch television set, she scanned the titles quickly. The space was shared by CDs, books and a handful of videos. None of her movies were among them. Instead, she noticed that each one was a rendition of a Shakespeare movie brought to the screen. Now that was a surprise. *The Hunk Who Liked Shakespeare.* Might make a good title for a mystery, she mused.

"Just go about your business." She turned around to look at him, her eyes sweeping over his torso in full appreciation. He'd lowered his weapon. Other things remained at attention. A smile spread across her lips. "Feel free to put away your gun. Pretend like I'm not here."

As if he could. Shaw looked at her, feeling as if he'd just been dared.

"Okay."

He placed his secondary weapon beside his service revolver on the shelf just above her head. As he reached up, he was so close to her, their bodies all but touched. Then, stepping back, he pulled his towel free of the knot that held it precariously in place. He had the satisfaction of seeing the pupils of her eyes dilate as her mouth fell open.

Shaw turned on his heel and started to walk back to the bathroom, his towel in his hand.

The inside of her mouth had turned to sawdust at the same time that her pulse sped up. The man looked incredible, coming *and* going. She had to remind herself to breathe.

"What—" Moira cleared her throat, trying to find the slightest evidence of saliva. There was none. The rest of her words dragged themselves along a bone-dry tongue. "What are you doing?" she finally managed to get out.

He glanced over his shoulder before walking into the bathroom. His voice might have been innocent, but his expression wasn't.

"Doing what you told me. Pretending like you're not here."

"Oh."

The moment she heard the bathroom door close, Moira spun on her heel and headed for his kitchen. She needed a glass of water.

Badly.

Chapter Four

After the performance he'd just given, Shaw was pretty confident that his uninvited guest would be gone by the time he finished showering and dressing.

She wasn't.

The woman wasn't anywhere in sight when he first opened his bathroom door, but there was a definite aroma in the air that hadn't been there before.

Eggs and coffee.

The aroma became stronger the closer he got to the kitchen.

So did the scent of her perfume. It was light and airy, yet very potent, which didn't make any sense to him, but he could detect it separately from the tempting aroma of food.

It surprised him that another, deeper hunger stirred, but then, he was only human, only male. And every so often, the fact that he wasn't in anything that could even remotely be called a relationship did rise up to take a bite out of him.

Talk about rotten timing.

The last person in the world he would want to suddenly feel male around was a movie star. As far as he was concerned, they were, by definition, a shallow breed in need of adulation and constant reaffirmation. That wasn't within his job description.

He'd never been a joiner per se and signing up to be part of Moira McCormick's fan club was as out of character, as foreign for him, as suddenly growing feathers and flying south for the winter.

He came into the kitchen. Not only did she have something going on the stove, but she seemed to be doing something with his refrigerator that involved a sponge and the garbage pail he kept hidden in the cabinet beneath the sink.

"What are you doing?"

He'd startled her and she jumped, pulling back and swinging around. Moira came within an inch of colliding with him. Reflexes had him grabbing for her before she made contact.

Holding her, Shaw realized that for all her bravado and the larger-than-life aura she cast, Moira

McCormick was rather a delicate woman, at least in structure.

He didn't release her as quickly as he should have. Deep green eyes looked up at him, amusement winking in and out.

"Cleaning out your refrigerator and making you breakfast with the only edible things I could find. Is there a lab paying you to house some of these things?"

She nodded at the pail that now held the take-out containers whose origin in time he couldn't begin to pinpoint. The pungent smell told him that their safety margin had long since expired.

He chose to ignore her flippant question. "I didn't know Hollywood types knew how to cook and clean."

Shaw couldn't begin to adequately describe the smile that played along her lips, only that it managed to pull him in. "I wasn't always a Hollywood type. Once I was a real person. Real people know how to do a whole lot of things. Sit."

He stayed where he was, watching as she moved the scrambled eggs from the pan to a plate. "I don't usually have breakfast at home."

She made her own interpretation. "This is better than grabbing a prefried egg sitting on a leathery muffin from some fast-food place, trust me." Moira set the plate down on the table.

He began to say that he ate breakfast with his family at his father's house, but that seemed like much too personal a piece of information to give her. And there was no way he was taking her over there with him. Last night had been all right, but awkward. Shaw had no idea how this morning would go. His father and the rest of the family had enough on their hands to cope with without adding this woman to the mix.

''Trust you,'' he echoed as he finally sat down at the table. She'd set only one place, but then, as he recalled, there were only two eggs left in the refrigerator and maybe she'd already eaten. Shaw moved the napkin and fork to the opposite side of the plate. ''Trust is something that's earned.'' His eyes met hers. ''I don't even know you.''

''That'll change,'' she promised cheerfully. She passed the sponge over the shelf, then tossed it into the sink. ''We'll get to know each other. Like I just got to know something about you.''

Shaw fully expected her to make some comment about the previous scene in his living room before he'd gone back to the shower. He braced himself. ''Like?''

''Like you're left-handed.'' Moira poured herself a cup of coffee, then sat down to face him. She took a sip before she continued. ''Did you know that left-handed people are now considered to be, on the average, more intelligent than right-handed people? Quite a comeback for a group that was thought of as the devil's spawn three hundred years ago. Shame they don't live as long as right-handed people.''

Shaw cocked his head, as if he was looking behind her. She turned her head, following his line of vision. There was nothing there. ‘‘What’s the matter?’’

‘‘Just looking for the key that wound you up.’’ The eggs were good and he hadn’t realized how hungry he was. ‘‘Are you just making this stuff up as you go along?’’

Moira savored the hot liquid for a moment before answering. ‘‘No. My father was left-handed.’’

‘‘Was?’’

‘‘Is,’’ she corrected. ‘‘I haven’t seen him for a while. We kind of lost track of each other.’’ And she missed him, she added silently, missed him terribly. But she’d given her father an ultimatum for his own good, saying she didn’t want to see him until he changed his ways. That had been almost two years ago, just before her career had skyrocketed. There’d been no word since then. She couldn’t help wondering if pride was keeping her father away from her.

Shaw made short work of his breakfast, but took time over his coffee. ‘‘Don’t see how that’s possible, seeing as how your face is everywhere.’’

‘‘I know,’’ she said quietly. ‘‘We didn’t exactly part on the best of terms.’’ She straightened her shoulders with renewed resolve. ‘‘He knows where to find me if he wants to.’’

Shaw knew he shouldn’t ask. The less he knew about this woman who had been pushed into his life, the better. More than likely, the parting of the ways she was referring to had come about because of something she'd done. In any case, it was none of his business.

But something in her voice wouldn't let him just leave it alone. He heard himself asking, "What kind of terms did you part on?"

"His," she said simply. And then she smiled that quicksilver smile of hers that was guaranteed to bring teenage boys to their knees and send teenage girls running to the nearest makeup counter in hopes of achieving the "Moira McCormick look."

Shaw realized he was staring and forced himself to look at his own coffee cup as if it held special interest for him. "So now you're being mysterious?"

"No, I'm being sensible." Her father had admonished her for being too open. *Don't let people in, Moira. That'll give them the upper hand and they can use it to hurt you.* "I've got a feeling that you're too much of a cop to hear any more."

Shaw thought of Hawk, Teri's partner, and what he had recently learned about his sister's fiancé's late parents. "Your father a drug dealer?"

Had she been drinking coffee, he would have been wearing it right now. As it was, Moira stared at him before she burst out laughing.

"Drugs? Oh, God, no." Her father was very strict about that. The only thing he had been strict about. "The only drug of choice my father believed in was wine—the more expensive, the better.'' She sighed just before draining her cup. ''That was the problem—he had very, very expensive tastes.''

She'd managed to hook him. He wanted answers. ''Then what? He's a burglar?''

Moira shook her head. ''My father separated people from their money with his tongue.'' A fond smile played on her lips. ''He could charm the fur off a snow leopard.''

Now he understood. Beneath her fancy description, her father was a common thief. ''A con man.''

''Artist,'' Moira corrected. Getting up, she got the coffeepot and divided what was left between their two cups. They got approximately three swallows each. ''A con *artist.*'' Retiring the pot to its burner, she sat down again, taking the cup between both hands. ''I always thought that if he had devoted his considerable brain power and abilities to something a little more traditional, my father would have been king by now.''

''We don't have kings,'' Shaw pointed out.

Her smile just grew. ''They would have made an exception for him.''

He paused, studying her. Drawing his own conclusions. ''But you didn't approve.''

She'd approved of her father, but once she was old enough to realize the dangers involved, divorcing them from the excitement that a successful score could generate, she'd no longer approved of the lifestyle he'd chosen. She didn't want him spending his remaining years in prison, which was where he was heading once his luck ran out. And eventually, everyone's luck ran out.

"My nerves weren't as steady as his," she explained evasively. "I thought of consequences." Her father never did. In a way, she supposed he was Peter Pan with a golden tongue. He'd never grown up. Fortunately, or unfortunately, she had. "I had a little more of my mother in me than my father."

Finished with his coffee, Shaw set down his cup. "Where is your mother?"

"Dead." She said the word crisply, refusing to unlock the pain that always emerged whenever she thought of her mother for more than a moment. "She died when I was seven. That's about the time when we hit the road." She smiled sadly to herself. "Up until the time Mama died, Daddy walked the straight and narrow. Had a nine-to-five job and everything."

She knew those times had been hard on him, but she would have given anything if things could have continued that way. It was the last time she'd felt secure. Safe. "I used to sit at the window, waiting for him to come home." She could almost see it in her mind's eye. "Every night, he'd come up that walk, looking like the weight of the world was on his shoulders. But the second he walked into the house, out came that thousand-watt smile. He really loved my mother a great deal, would have done anything for her."

Sorrow threatened to overpower her. Moira struggled to stay one step ahead of it, divorcing herself from her past, pretending it was only a character she was talking about, not her father, not someone who mattered the world to her.

"Broke his heart when he lost her. He sold the house, sold everything that reminded him of her."

"How did you go to school?"

The question only made her smile widen as memories returned to her. "For the most part, at the University of Daddy." She could see that the answer didn't sit well with Shaw. "When the time came," she assured him, "I took an equivalency test. Passed with flying colors, too." He looked surprised. She realized that she liked surprising him. "Like I said, my father was very, very smart." There was still skepticism in his eyes. "Ask me anything."

He wasn't about to play a lightning round of Jeop ardy with her. In his experience, people didn't put out challenges like that unless they could live up to them. Besides, there was something else he wanted to know about her. "What made you get into acting?"

It wasn't the question she'd expected. She thought he'd take special pleasure in trying to find a question she couldn't answer. "Natural transition, I guess. I was used to pretending."

He came to the only conclusion he could. "Your father used you in his scams?"

He made it sound so sordid. It hadn't been anything of the kind. They'd lived in some of the best hotels, and she and Carrie had never wanted for anything. Except, maybe for the traditional life they'd lost.

In response, she shook her head. The maternal feelings that had her looking after her father as well as her sister kept her from answering his question.

"See, I told you you were too much of a policeman to hear this. It wasn't your jurisdiction, Detective. No sense in getting worked up." She nodded at his empty plate. "So, how was it?"

He glanced down at the plate and raised a shoulder in a half shrug. "Not bad."

Moira splayed her hand across her chest and rolled her eyes heavenward. "Oh, please, sir, you flatter me too much."

He didn't know whether to be irritated or amused. He settled for a mixture of both. "Okay, good. It was good. Satisfied?"

"It'll do. For now." Rising, she picked up both cups and the dish. Instead of depositing them in the sink and leaving them there the way he would have, Shaw watched her wash the cups and plate, then set them on the rack to dry. Since there was no dish towel available, she dried her hands off on the back of her jeans, then turned around to face him.

"Now what do you do?"

He frowned, aware that he'd watched her—a bit too intently—wipe her hands off. "Wonder how the hell I got myself into this."

She stood over him. Cutting into his space. "Besides that."

He glanced at his watch. Instead of answering, he got up and strode to the phone. He flipped open the small phone book he had beside it. Finding his brother's new number, he tapped it out on the cordless receiver, then waited for Clay to pick up.

He got the answering machine instead.

"Damn," he muttered, hanging up. So much for shooting hoops. He'd waited too long to call. Clay was probably already on his way to the house.

Moira came up behind him. "Anything I can help with?"

He spoke before he could censor himself. "Not unless you know how to play basketball."

The moment the words were out, he saw her smiling broadly at him. What?

"This is your lucky day," she informed him

Right. She could play competitively. There was more to basketball than pretending to be a player. "You're only, what, five-two?"

Moira drew herself up a little. "Five-four and a half." She saw that the increased height had no effect on him. "One stick of dynamite can do a lot more damage than a charging rhino."

What was *that* supposed to mean? "Neither of which is known for its skill with a basketball," he pointed out. His eyes narrowed as he regarded her. "You expect me to believe you play basketball?"

"No, I expect you to come to that conclusion after

we do a little one-on-one. That was what you were trying to do, wasn't it, find someone to shoot a few hoops with you?'' she guessed, then spread her arms out wide. ''Well, here I am.''

Yes, here she was, he thought darkly. A five-foot-four-and-a-half blond thorn in his side. He supposed the best way to get her to stop was to play her. ''Okay, you're on.''

He led the way to the door. ''Want to make a little wager on the side to make it interesting?'' she asked as they walked out of the apartment.

About to shut the door behind them, Shaw stopped dead and looked at her. ''Is that how you did it?''

He'd lost her. ''Did what?''

''Rope people in for one of your father's con games?''

Though she was protective of her father, she took no offense. ''My father never hustled basketball,'' she informed him. Then she added, ''Times were tough. He hustled pool, but never basketball.''

As if that made everything all right. Shaw shook his head. ''I'll consider myself forewarned.''

She was as good as her word.

Bringing her to a local park, Shaw lost no time in getting started. He figured that at least he'd get a workout and burn a few calories. He didn't expect her to play well enough to give him a run for his money.

She didn't play basketball. She owned the game. For a small woman, he quickly discovered, Moira McCormick had more moves than a team of semi-pros. She stunned him by being all over the court and making him work for every point he scored.

He'd begun by trying to take it easy on her. After all, that was what males did with females, he reasoned. They went easy on them. He'd learned a long time ago that the average woman was nothing like one of his sisters. The average woman wasn't competitive and she wasn't incredibly athletic.

But, he quickly learned, Moira McCormick was not the average woman. Certainly not the average movie star.

She was good.

She was better than good.

She took his breath away—and the ball—whenever possible. Which was often.

Time melted away as they played. All he could focus on was the game.

And the woman.

"Had enough?" she asked, panting as she made another basket.

The sound of her breathing heavily was getting to him. And it had nothing to do with his spirit of competition. It was evoking a completely different scenario in his head. One he was trying desperately not to acknowledge.

Besides, it was getting late. If he was going to get

to the precinct on time, he had to stop now and start getting ready.

Still, he didn't want to call it off. Not when he was losing. Shaw looked at her grudgingly. "Game's not over."

With a quick nod of her head, Moira assumed a ready stance, her legs spread apart, her body poised. "Fine with me."

Desire, strong, red-blooded and able, roared through his veins with a speed that astounded him. He needed another shower, a colder one this time. Not that he really thought it would help. This was going to take a little mind over matter.

Maybe more than a little mind over matter, he silently amended.

He looked at his watch again. He *really* had to get going. "Rest of the game has to be postponed," he informed her. "I'm due at work."

"*We're* due at work," Moira corrected. She blew out a breath, then drew another one in.

He found himself watching, fascinated, as her lungs expanded. The glimmer of a grin on her lips told him that he'd been caught at it.

"Good game," she commented. They started walking back to his apartment.

It was one of his better ones, but it still hadn't been good enough. "I was a little off."

"Yes, I noticed." He looked at her sharply. She laughed, shaking her head. "Don't kid around much, do you?"

He didn't like the way she seemed to think she could read his mind. "With my friends."

He lengthened his stride. She followed suit, stretching to keep up. "How long does it take to get into this exclusive club?"

He spared her one glance that was meant to cut her off at the knees. Whatever game she was playing, he wanted no part of.

"Why would you want to be my friend?"

"Why not?" she countered, refusing to be intimidated. Better men than he had tried their hand at that and she had never flinched. Part of the education she'd sustained at her father's knee. "I've always found it's nicer to have friends than to go it alone in life."

"So you can fleece them?"

She stopped walking. He found himself turning around even as he told himself to keep going. "Don't make me regret being honest with you, Shaw. I don't like having regrets."

"Welcome to the club," he muttered. Then he added, "Sorry, that was uncalled for." He normally didn't take cheap shots like that. What was getting into him?

They'd reached his complex. He looked around, but didn't see anything that might have passed for the kind of car he figured a celebrity of her status would drive. "Where's your car?"

"At the hotel where I'm staying. I had a driver drop me off. I figured you'd do the honors."

"Would have been nice to have been asked."

If she'd asked ahead of time, she knew what the answer would have been. And it would have interfered with her goal to grow on him. So, instead, she got into his face now and batted her eyelashes at him in silent-screen-star fashion. "Would you?"

"A little late for that, isn't it?"

"Better late than never."

"C'mon," he growled, waving her toward his car.

Moira didn't wait for a second invitation. She prided herself on being able to read people, and Detective Cavanaugh of the vice squad had all the signs of a man who, given half a chance, could take off without her.

She wasn't about to give him that chance.

Chapter Five

The silence in the car was far from comfortable. Waiting for Shaw to say the first word was tantamount to waiting for snow to make an appearance in the desert. It just wasn't going to happen.

She wondered what it would take for him to feel more relaxed around her. Having basketball in common certainly hadn't done it for him.

Studying his rigid profile for a moment, Moira played another card. "You don't remember me, do you?"

Shaw spared her a quick glance as he drove through the intersection. "I'm a little young for Alzheimer's," he retorted sarcastically, then stated the obvious. ''You're the woman from the movies, the one who got lucky on the basketball court.''

She laughed and it bothered him that the sound got under his skin, irritating him because it seemed so inviting.

''Luck had nothing to do with it,'' she told him glibly. ''Skill, however, did. But I'm not talking about any of that. Think back.''

Shaw frowned. He had never liked games. ''How far back?''

''Tenth grade. Half of tenth grade, actually.'' She could see that he wasn't buying into this. ''Mrs. Alma Brickman's Speech class.''

His eyes narrowed. How the hell did she know his teacher's name? This wasn't some lucky guess on her part. You didn't pluck a name like Alma Brickman out of the air. As far as he knew, that kind of information wasn't readily available.

''What do you know about Mrs. Brickman?''

She closed her eyes for a second, summoning the woman's image. It helped to be gifted with total recall. Her father certainly had gloried in her gift. ''Short, gray hair, kindly voice.'' Moira opened her eyes again to see how he was taking this in. ''She had us act out scenes from plays. Shakespeare, mostly. I noticed by the videos on your shelf, she got you at least partially hooked.''

The light turned red. He stepped on the brake and turned to stare at her. She'd described his speech teacher to a T. As far as he knew, there was only one way she could have known.

"You were in my class?"

Moira nodded, satisfied that she had managed to shake him up a little. "All of five months."

At this point, most of high school was a haze. He tried to summon her face out of the crowd and failed. It had to be a put-on. But if it was, how had she known about his teacher?

"I don't remember you."

Small wonder there. She'd been a late bloomer. His girlfriend, however, hadn't been. "That's because at the time you were going with Monica Zale." Her mouth curved. "A cheerleader who always brought along her own set of pom-poms."

Monica Zale. The name took him back. He hadn't thought of Monica in years. The perky brunette had been the best-endowed girl in the tenth grade. Or any other grade for that matter. They'd gone together for a year and a half until he realized that looks were definitely not enough. He needed someone with a brain to talk to. That someone hadn't turned out to be Monica.

The light turned green. And then he remembered. "I thought you said you were homeschooled."

"For the most part," she allowed. "I begged my father to let me enroll in a regular school." When he'd finally agreed, she'd thought the wandering was behind them. "I thought that maybe he was finally going to settle down." And for a time, he had. Until the lure of another con got the better of him. ''But things got a little warm and we had to pick up stakes and go.'' There'd been arguments then. Real arguments. They weren't little kids anymore, she and her sister, willingly being led from place to place as if it was all a big adventure. She shook her head, remembering. ''Carrie was really teed-off at him.''

He turned off the main thoroughfare. ''Carrie?''

''My sister.'' She stopped, trying to remember. ''Did I not mention her?''

He shrugged carelessly. ''Maybe you did and I wasn't listening.'' But he knew she hadn't. Even against his will, he took in all information that came his way and processed it. And Moira had sent a lot of information his way. ''Anyone else in your family?''

''No, just the three of us. My sister, Carrie, is a year younger than me.'' Although at times, it felt as if she were a whole generation older. Carrie had been like their father, accustomed to getting her own way, never really growing up to take on the responsibilities of an adult. More than once, Moira had felt as if she were mother to both of them. ''She took off for parts unknown about a year before Dad and I came to a parting of the ways.'' A fond, sad smile played along her lips. ''Carrie was always the stubborn one.''

Shaw thought of Rayne, of the grief she'd given their father before finally settling down. The comment came out before he could think to stop it. "Got one of those myself."

He was sharing. She wondered if he realized that. "I'd like to meet her sometime."

Shaw nodded, but made no commitment. Besides, they were here, at the precinct. And his day, he thought with a heavy, inward sigh, was just beginning.

As he pulled into the parking lot, he thought he saw his partner. At first, he thought something was up, but then he realized the man was just being impatient.

Reese leaned against the hood of his car, his head moving slowly from side to side like some kind of searchlight. The moment his head turned in their direction and he saw them, Reese came to attention. He immediately made his way over to them.

Shaw barely got a chance to pull into his parking space before Reese was opening up Moira's door. His attention was completely focused on the celebrity.

"Here's your fan club," Shaw muttered.

"I think he's sweet," she told him, flashing her brilliant smile at Reese.

Shaw pulled up the hand brake. "That's Reese," he growled. "Sweet."

"Hi." Extending his hand, Reese helped her out of the passenger side. As far as Shaw was concerned, his partner was smiling at her like a lovesick puppy. ''I was afraid that yesterday was just a wistful dream.''

Shaw closed his own door. ''No such luck,'' he muttered.

Reese continued holding her hand, obviously mesmerized by her appearance even though she'd tried to play down her looks. ''Are you ready to get started, Ms. McCormick? Or would you like to go inside to freshen up first?''

''It's Moira,'' she corrected.

''Moira.'' Reese sighed the name.

Shaw clutched his stomach like a man trying not to throw up. ''Too bad we've only got shower stalls available or you could draw her a bath, too.''

Reese frowned at his partner. Belatedly, he released Moira's hand, then fell into step beside her as the three of them headed for the front steps of the building. ''Don't pay any attention to him, he's a barbarian.''

In a way, the description fit, she thought. Shaw Cavanaugh did have a little of the barbarian in him. And it was damn sexy at that. ''I know all about Shaw Cavanaugh.''

''Oh?'' Surprised, Reese looked from Moira to Shaw. ''Did I miss something?''

Moira gave Shaw first chance to say something. When he didn't, she was more than happy to fill the other detective in. ''I went to school here for five months. Shaw was in my class.''

Reese looked accusingly at Shaw. ''Why didn't you tell me?''

Shaw yanked the door open. He didn't bother looking at Reese. ''I didn't know.''

Thunderstruck, Reese could only stare at Moira. ''How could you not know?''

Shaw walked into the building ahead of the other two. This had the makings of a very long day. ''Can we just get started?'' he growled.

Reese inclined his head conspiratorially toward Moira. ''My partner's kind of grumpy until he has his morning coffee.''

''He's had his morning coffee,'' Moira told him. Her remark was met with more surprise. She held up two fingers. ''Two cups.''

Again, Reese's brown eyes slid from the back of Shaw's head to Moira's face. ''And you'd know this how?''

''She made it,'' Shaw tossed over his shoulder as he headed for the stairwell and the second-floor squad room where he clocked in every morning.

This was almost too much to digest. ''You made his coffee?'' Reese's voice was filled with wonder and a touch of envy. ''Why?''

She hurried up the metal stairs behind Shaw. ''I wanted some, too.''

Reese reached the landing with her. ''Can we start at the beginning here?''

As Shaw held open the door, she walked out onto the second floor and to what appeared to be an audience that had been milling around for a while now, waiting for her to make an appearance. Her eyes swept over the crowd and she smiled at every last one of them.

"We've got all day," she told Reese cheerfully.

Shaw's look only grew darker.

The morning had been filled with details and phone calls he wouldn't allow her to overhear. She'd spent it talking to some of the other detectives and waiting for some sign that Shaw and Reese were about to spring into action.

When they started to walk out, she hurried to catch up. Reese looked happy about it. Shaw did not.

They were on their way to check out a tip. Despite what his uncle had said, despite the agreement the city and Moira's studio had reached, Shaw was against her tagging along. As far as he was concerned, having Moira there put all of their lives in danger. Especially hers.

He gave her as few details as he could get away with. They were going to check out a pornography store downtown. Someone had tipped them off that there was a distant connection between the owner and the prostitution ring they were trying to bring down.

When he pulled up to the curb, he grabbed Moira's wrist as she started to unbuckle her seat belt. She raised her eyes to his face questioningly. ''I want you to stay in the car.''

She felt a flash of temper, but banked it down. ''But how am I going to see you in action if I have to stay in the car?''

He got out, slamming the door. The look he gave her pinned her to her seat. ''Use your imagination.''

Moira frowned. ''I could have stayed in the hotel and done that.''

''Now there's an idea.''

Moira turned her eyes toward her only ally. Reese was quick to pick up the banner. ''She's got a point, Shaw. Why don't you let her come along?''

This was nonnegotiable. ''She's a civilian and she could get hurt. She stays where she is.''

Fun was fun, but this was getting in the way of her research. ''But—''

He decided to try to appeal to her common sense, even though he wasn't sure if she had any. ''Look, we're entering a sleazy place that deals exclusively in explicit porno.'' He didn't add that there was a suspicion of child pornography being produced out of there, as well. He wasn't trying to make her ill, just make her stay put. ''Men go into places like that, not women. Having you with us'll blow our cover.''

Moira looked undaunted. ''I could play the part of a wanna-be porn star.''

The woman had an answer for everything. He lost his temper. Shaw leaned into the car. When he spoke, he enunciated every word. "Let's get something clear. There are no *'parts'* here. These are not TV actors we're dealing with. They don't retreat into their trailers when someone yells 'Cut.' These are vicious, nasty men who sell underage girls into virtual slavery. Now this is as close as you're getting to the operation." He slapped the side of the car. "Do I make myself clear?"

There was no arguing with him. "Perfectly."

"Good." Shaw straightened up. "I'm glad we're on the same page."

He looked at his partner. Reese had changed inside the precinct, donning worn jeans and a pullover shirt that had seen too many spin cycles in the washing machine. The object was to blend in, not stand out.

Shaw felt behind him, assuring himself that his weapon was still tucked into the waistband of his jeans at the small of his back. The one he used for backup was securely strapped to his calf.

Completely ignoring Moira, he nodded at Reese. "Okay, let's do this."

Frustrated, Moira remained in the car.

She watched Shaw and Reese as they disappeared behind the black door of a small, narrow store whose display windows had been painted black. If what was going on inside was what Shaw claimed, black was an appropriate color for it, she thought.

They were gone a while.

The minutes dragged one another by in slow motion, making her edgy. The interior of the car began to get warmer despite the windows that were cracked open on either side. She stood it for as long as she could. Finally, feeling as if she were in a rotisserie, Moira slid into the driver's seat and looked around for a way to open the windows all the way down.

But Shaw had taken the keys with him and she needed the keys to operate the power windows.

"Terrific," she muttered. "He did this on purpose so that I'd call this off. Guess what, Shaw. I'm a lot tougher than you think." She blew out a breath, watching the front of the porno store. "Also a lot hotter."

Moira gave it a few more minutes, growing warmer, antsier by the moment. But there was no sign of either Reese or Shaw. No movement whatsoever in the general area.

The interior of the car grew hotter.

She debated getting out of the vehicle, but she knew that wouldn't sit well with Shaw. Besides, she thought, looking around at the tired buildings, the dirty streets, this wasn't exactly an upscale neighborhood. She might be stubborn, but she wasn't an idiot.

Moira chewed on her lower lip, thinking. She wiped the perspiration from her forehead. There was only one thing left to do.

She was going to have to hot-wire the car in order to get the windows down.

Leaning over, she got busy beneath the dashboard. It had been a while since she'd done anything like this, but it was like riding a bicycle. After a few seconds of fumbling, it came back to her.

Several short tries later, she had the engine purring like a kitten.

Smiling, feeling triumphant, Moira straightened up. She spread her fingers out over the buttons on the driver's armrest and pushed all the four that were clustered together. All four windows began to dip down in unison.

It was then she saw the door to the porno shop open. Less than a half beat later, a man came flying out. He was running as if he had the demons from hell on his tail. She figured two police detectives were close enough, given his probable line of work.

Later, looking back, she didn't recall thinking, only reacting. Years of being her father's daughter, ready for anything, had honed her reflexes to a razor-fine point.

She threw the car into drive and aimed it directly for the man Shaw and Reese were pursuing.

Running at top speed, Shaw's eyes widened as he saw the car whizzing by him. The fact that it was his registered a moment later.

Pumping hard behind him, Reese's mouth dropped opened. "Hey, isn't that—?"

"Damn it. What the hell does she think she's doing?" By the time the question was out, he had his answer.

Driving over the curb, Moira had brought the cream-colored Crown Victoria up on the sidewalk. For a second, it looked as if she were going to run the man down, but she brought the vehicle to a halt, effectively pinning the terrified quarry up against the wall.

"Hey, nicely done!" Reese called out to her as he and Shaw rushed to catch up.

Shaw saw no reason to praise her. What she did was reckless and dangerous. If the shop owner had had a gun, she could have gotten herself killed.

"What do you—? How did you—?" He couldn't even frame a question. They went spilling into each other, shoved forward by indignation, surprise and anger.

Excited, Moira didn't even hear Shaw at first. She leaped out of the car to take a closer look at the man she'd caught. Her heart was pounding. It had been a long time since she'd felt this alive. In a way, she supposed she missed the life she'd once led with her father and sister.

"She's crazy!" the store owner screamed. "Why don't you arrest her?"

"We're too busy with you," Reese told him, taking out his cuffs.

His hand on her shoulder, Shaw spun Moira around to face him. The look on her face was sheer exhilaration and for a second, his indignation faded. But it was back the next moment.

"What the hell do you think you're doing?" he demanded.

"Helping."

Shaw looked accusingly at Reese. The latter had turned the store owner toward the wall and was snapping the handcuffs shut. "Did you leave the keys in the car?"

Reese shook his head. "Hey, man, you drove, remember?"

Shaw felt his pocket. The keys were still there. Then how did she—?

Moira read the question in his eyes. "I hot-wired it. It was hot," she explained. "I didn't know how long you'd be and I was trying to get the windows down before I wound up roasting to death." She shrugged innocently. "I figured you wouldn't want me getting out of the car."

It took a lot of willpower to keep his temper under control. "I didn't want you racing the car, either."

Why was he so annoyed? She'd helped, not hindered. "I saw you running after someone. He was getting away."

"I would have caught him."

She smiled up at him, satisfied with herself. "My way was faster."

He was going to get rid of her if it was the last thing he did. "Your way was damn dangerous."

Handcuffed, the suspect was craning his neck as Reese tried to get him into the back seat. Outrage and fear had temporarily been replaced by curiosity. The man looked at Reese. ''Hey, is that—?''

''Moira McCormick,'' Moira said. Despite the circumstances, she added, ''Nice to meet you.''

Shaw roughly took hold of her arm, escorting Moira back into the car. ''You can sign autographs later,'' he growled.

''This isn't going to work,'' he said to her several minutes later. She was in the front seat with him. Reese was in the back with the suspect, who hadn't stopped talking to her since he realized who she was.

Moira turned back around and looked at Shaw. She'd obeyed him and remained in the car, and still managed to help out. What more did he want? ''I thought it worked out just fine.''

''You thought wrong. I told you to stay in the car.''

''At no time did my body leave the car,'' she protested. ''Not until after you were on the scene.''

He knew it was useless to argue with her. She'd just infuriate him. Shaw blew out a breath, trying to collect himself.

''Where did you learn to do that?'' Reese asked, admiration in his voice.

She knew he was referring to hot-wiring. Her father had taught both her and her sister how. It was something he thought might be useful to them someday. He'd only stolen one car during his career. It had belonged to a man who'd gotten rich off the misfortune of others. Her father had called it "payback." Eventually, the car had been donated to a charity.

"Research," she lied. Moira exchanged looks with Shaw. It became evident to him that although she'd told him about her father and the life they'd led in the shadow of the wrong side of the law, it seemed to be something that she didn't want to become common knowledge.

Or maybe she'd put him on this morning and what she'd just told Reese was the truth. Maybe she'd been so busy pretending that she no longer knew what was true and what wasn't.

None of which mattered to him.

All that mattered was that he had to get this shapely, attractive monkey off his back and the sooner he did that, the better.

"So, are you going to interrogate him?" she asked. When he made no answer, she tried again. "C'mon, Cavanaugh, I didn't hurt the car."

"That's not the point. You could have gotten hurt—"

"Ah, you care."

He glared at her. "About the city getting sued because you want to play cops and robbers—yes, I care."

She seemed to accept his explanation. "Don't worry. I already signed a disclaimer. I get hurt—nobody's liable but me."

Somehow, that didn't seem to comfort him the way he thought it should.

Chapter Six

"You probably won't let me in there with you, will you?"

Moira looked from Shaw to Reese, knowing it was a dead issue.

Though he and Reese were partners, Shaw was definitely the leader here, and she knew he would never bend the rules to allow her inside the interrogation room while they questioned Ramsey Jenkins, the porno shop owner she'd helped capture.

Shaw tossed his jacket over the back of his chair and rolled up his sleeves. It was hot inside the precinct and it would get a lot hotter in the room where the suspect was being kept. "Give the lady a prize, Reese. She guessed the right answer."

Reese bit his lower lip as Moira looked at him again. "Cavanaugh...?"

"No." The answer was firm and nonnegotiable.

"Don't you have a little room behind the one you use for interrogations? You know, one of those places with a one-way mirror? So I can see but not be seen?" she tacked on hopefully. "I'm not some police groupie, Shaw. I need to study your technique." She glanced toward Reese for backup. She wasn't disappointed.

"C'mon, Cavanaugh. What's the harm in letting her watch?"

Shaw gave him a dirty look. He didn't like being observed, didn't like anything about this overall assignment, but he knew he was on the losing side. She'd probably go to the chief, and that was the last thing he wanted.

He looked down at her. "Okay, but no tapping on the window, no sudden movements, no indication that you're there. Understand?"

She held up her hand, as if she was taking an oath. "I won't even breathe."

"That," he muttered under his breath, "is too much to hope for."

"C'mon," Reese urged, beckoning to her. "I'll show you where to go."

The look on Shaw's face, she noticed, indicated

that he would have liked to tell her *exactly* where to go. She hurried after Reese.

Moira stood, fascinated, as she watched Shaw patiently, quietly, firmly grill the porno shop owner. It wasn't like in the movies. She wasn't sure just what she'd expected. Maybe a game of good cop–bad cop, or maybe she'd thought that Shaw would flex his prowess over the man, threaten him with bodily harm then give him just enough of a taste of it to have him babbling out the information.

But Shaw went about his grilling methodically. He was a man with a goal in mind and would not stop until that goal was reached. Reese was there solely for reinforcement. The longer the questioning continued, the more uneasy Jenkins became.

In the end, faced with the threat of being sent to prison, Jenkins finally talked. If convicted, this would have marked his third offense, guaranteeing him a life behind bars. Begging them to say it hadn't come from him, Jenkins gave them the name of his connection.

They had another piece of the puzzle.

Highly impressed, Moira came out of the adjoining room just as Shaw emerged. "That was fantastic."

He gestured to another detective to take the prisoner to a holding cell. It had gone well in there. Sometimes it didn't. Still there was no reason to celebrate yet.

Shaw merely shrugged, his attention for the most part focused on the information Jenkins had given them. But it was hard not to take note of the brilliant smile on Moira's face. A smile that somehow found its way into his gut.

He was tired and wired at the same time and in no condition to be around a sparkling Hollywood player. Almost in self-defense, he glanced at his watch. "It's late. Isn't it about time you went back to your sound stage, or big party, or wherever it is that you go?"

She was being dismissed, but took no offense since she was getting used to his abrupt behavior. "Actually, there is a party," she told him. "A pre-cast party. My producer is throwing it for the cast and crew." She looked at him pointedly. "That includes the technical advisers."

So that was the title they'd slapped on him and Reese. He raised an eyebrow, amused despite himself. "You want my advice?"

Moira had a strong hunch she knew what it would be. She grinned at him. "Not at this moment, no. But I'll let you know when the time comes. Anyway, you and Reese are invited." She nodded toward Reese. "So's your chief, if he'd like to come."

Shaw didn't know about his uncle, but he knew that he didn't want to go. As he began to turn her down, Reese, apparently suddenly blessed with clairvoyance, grabbed his arm and pulled him aside.

"C'mon," he entreated, lowering his voice to just

below a stage whisper. "What harm would it do? Think of it as a few hours to unwind. We could all use that," Reese urged, his eyes dancing hopefully back and forth across Shaw's face. "How many chances do we have to go to a real Hollywood-type party?"

"Nobody's stopping you." Shaw pulled his arm away. "What do you need me for?"

"Backup," Reese stressed. "Besides, it's not me she's looking at."

Yes, he was aware that there had been eye contact. Aware, too, that there might have been a few other things going on, all without any nurturing on his part. He supposed it could have been referred to by some as chemistry. The kind that blew up labs, not the kind that created useful, beneficial things for mankind. "She's absorbing the part."

Reese laughed shortly. "She's absorbing you," he corrected, then temporarily lost his endless supply of patience. "What the hell's the matter with you? If I had a chance to be with a beautiful woman like that—"

"Yeah, we all know what you'd do." The answer was all over Reese's love-struck face.

Shaw frowned, thinking. Maybe he was attaching too much importance to all of this. Yes, it was an inconvenience and a pain in the butt, but in a couple of weeks, it would all be forgotten. By then the crew would have packed up and gone back to Los Angeles and the confines of a welcoming studio, leaving behind only their money to remind anyone that they had passed through—and some celluloid once the movie was released.

He supposed it wouldn't do any harm to go. Especially if his uncle was attending. He knew without being told that Brian would expect him to put in an appearance at the party if he was asked. And he'd been asked.

With a shrug that was the sheer definition of careless, Shaw raised his voice and looked back at Moira. "All right. Where and when?"

She crossed to him, pleased. "Wow, I didn't expect it to be this easy." She beamed at Reese, knowing he'd been behind it. "Jonathan's reserved the Green Ballroom at the hotel."

The name meant nothing to him. Was it supposed to? "Jonathan?"

"Jonathan Daley." She realized that still had no meaning for him. "Sorry. He's the producer."

"Why are you sorry?"

Moira dragged her hand through her hair. She wanted a bath—a long, lovely, hot bath—but she'd settle for a shower. Time was short. "Because I just did what I swore I'd never been guilty of doing." She saw his blank expression. Any second now, it would be chased away by impatience. "Name-dropping," she explained. "It's just that it's hard not to...."

Moira let her voice trail off, knowing there was no good way to end this sentence. There were times she wished she had her father's glib tongue. Matthew McCormick could always explain his way out of things.

That was just the problem. The more time that went by, the more certain she became that her father was using up his supply of luck and that someday, when it ran out, terrible things would happen to him. But he'd only laugh and tease her about worrying like an old woman. Eventually, not wanting to be there for the fateful day when it finally found him, she'd left.

Right now, she decided to concentrate on her minor victory. "Would you like me to send a car for you?" She looked from one man to the other.

Reese nodded, but Shaw wasn't so easily led along. "Why? Something wrong with my car?"

Why did he always gravitate to the negative side? "No. I just thought you might want to impress someone with a limo."

"There's no one to impress," he told her flatly.

Okay, so maybe she was digging. He obviously didn't live with anyone, but that didn't mean that Mr. Sunshine wasn't involved with someone. She cocked her head. "No one?"

"No one."

She tried to sound innocent as she regained ground. "Then you'll be driving in on your own?"

"Been driving since I was sixteen. See no reason to suddenly stop now just because I've got an invitation to a crew party."

"Precast party," she corrected automatically. "Then I'll see you there." She made an effort to look at both of them, and even to smile at Reese, but her attention was clearly on the taller of the two men. "Oh—" she realized that she'd told them the where, but not the when "—it's at eight."

"We'll be there with bells on," Reese promised. Turning away as Moira left, he let out a low whistle. "Man, do I wish I was you right now."

"Why?" He began to head back to his desk. There was a report to file before he could leave tonight. "You're invited, too. The only reason I'm going is because you want me to."

Reese trailed after him, a dreamy, puppy-dog expression on his face. "Yeah, but she didn't look at me the way she looked at you."

In the squad room, Shaw headed straight for his desk, avoiding making eye contact. He wasn't in the mood for questions. "And what way would that be?"

"Like she's got a yen for corn beef and you're the last corn-beef sandwich on the shelf."

Sinking down in his seat, he looked at his partner incredulously. "Where the hell do you get these thoughts from?"

Reese loosened his tie. "Doesn't matter where I get them from. What matters is that she looks like she's got a thing for you."

Shaw snorted. "She's an actress. They get a 'thing' for anyone."

The explanation obviously did not seem to deter Reese. ''Maybe, but she got it for you.''

He found that his patience was severely limited tonight. ''You don't know what the hell you're talking about, and if you keep on talking, I'm not going.''

Reese held his hands up in surrender. For all of five seconds, his computer commanded his attention. And then he looked up across the two desks that were butted up against each other. ''Hey, Cavanaugh?''

''Now what?'' Raising his eyes, Shaw gave him his most malevolent look.

''What are you gonna be wearing tonight?''

He clamped down on the temptation to use a ripe curse. Instead ''Clothes'' was all he said as he looked back down at his work, shaking his head.

Two hours later, on his way out the door of his small apartment, Shaw paused for a moment, his eyes on the wall phone.

He debated all of six seconds.

And then he was dialing, tapping out the familiar numbers to his sister Callie's apartment rather than his father's house.

She picked up on the third ring. One more and he knew he would have gotten the answering machine, which would have been his cue to hang up. Other than using them for undercover work, he had no patience for recording devices.

"Callie?"

"Shaw? What's wrong?"

He knew she was asking because he rarely called.

"Nothing. I just wanted to know how it was going. With Dad and—her," he tacked on.

They both knew who he was referring to. "Why don't you call him yourself?"

"Because I'm calling you, that's why."

Callie's voice indicated that she took no offense at his attitude. "You know, big brother, someday you're going to find out you can't just carry around your emotions in a neatly labeled package. Dad would appreciate hearing from you. He needs all the moral support he can get right now."

If he didn't like to be watched, he liked being analyzed even less, even by a woman he dearly loved. "Why? He was right. He found her. What's the problem?"

Callie's sigh almost screamed, *Boy, men can be so dumb.* "You know why. The 'why' is the reason you're calling and asking how things were going. The problem is that she's not whole. Because something happened to her to make her drive off that bridge."

"They had an argument."

"Lots of people have arguments. They don't drive off bridges into the river. Mom wasn't some flighty woman. She was stable."

He could only guess at the direction her mind was heading. "And you think if all that, the argument and her storming out of the house, was out in the open, she'd have her memory back?''

Callie sighed. ''I don't know. It's hard to tell,'' she admitted. ''I just know this is eating Dad up. He has her but he doesn't have her. Until her memory comes back, she's like some stranger with Mom's face.''

He noticed that Callie had said ''until.'' There was a hopeful ring in her voice. Though grounded in common sense, she was definitely the more upbeat of the two of them. He envied her that. That and a whole lot more, including her happiness. He hoped that this time it would really work out for her.

''If anyone can make her remember, it's Dad.''

There was a pause on the other end of the line, as if she was debating something. He certainly hadn't said anything very profound, he thought. Just as he was about say goodbye and hang up, he heard her.

''Shaw?''

''What?''

''Come by the house tomorrow.''

He knew she meant that it would be a show of support. Their father had always been there for them, no matter what. Even when Rayne gave him so much trouble, he never turned his back on her, never gave up. And he needed them all now in his corner.

It was the right thing to do and he knew it. ''Yeah.'' And then he hung up.

He had a party hanging over his head like some double-edged sword, and if he didn't show up, he knew he'd never hear the end of it from Reese. With a sigh, he left.

He felt like an outsider looking in.

The sensation descended over him the moment he walked in. The festively decorated ballroom was filled with people, all of whom seemed to know one another. Which left him out.

When faced with what he knew had been a similar situation at the precinct, Moira had waltzed into the middle of it and held court. But she was outgoing, gregarious. He wasn't; he never had been. They were a world apart in every way.

Looking around, he saw Reese. His partner was clearly in his element and loving it. He was in the middle of a group of very young, very nubile-looking women. Scanning the faces, Shaw found that he didn't recognize any of them, but that didn't mean anything. He'd hardly recognized Moira at first.

As he looked around the ballroom, he saw his uncle, standing not too far from Reese, engaged in a conversation with an earnest-looking older man. His uncle seemed to be enjoying himself.

Shaw wondered how long he would have to stay before he could leave.

"Wine, sir?"

He glanced to his side and saw a waitress standing

there, holding a tray filled with wineglasses and waiting for him to make a selection. There appeared to be three different kinds of wines to choose from.

"If you'd prefer something a little stronger, there's an open bar."

The suggestion came from behind him. One day in her presence and he already recognized her voice.

Moira.

"Wine's fine," he told her, making an arbitrary selection.

He wasn't much for wine, but it would give him something to do with his hands. Anything stronger might go straight to his head. He hadn't had much to eat today. The last thing he wanted was to feel intoxicated and make a fool of himself around her.

He was feeling damn awkward as it was. Searching for something to say, Shaw turned around. The moment he looked at her, he found that his tongue had been nailed to the roof of his mouth.

When he finally managed to pry it loose, he mumbled, "Dressmaker run out of material?"

Moira had on a hot pink, shimmery two-piece outfit. The top ended before it came to her waist, exposing a midriff that was taut, firm and tempting. The slightly flared skirt began somewhere below her navel and came halfway down her thighs, enough to cover everything, not enough to keep most men from a meltdown. The bottom of the skirt moved invitingly from side to side with each step she took. Her strapless sandals sported four-inch heels.

Looking down at her legs—just how long were they?—he couldn't decide whether she was wearing stockings, or if her legs were bare and incredibly tanned.

He knew he wanted to find out.

He was holding his wineglass a little too tightly, he realized. It was in self-defense. There was a sudden desire to run his hands along her legs so that he could make the final analysis himself.

She turned around in front of him slowly, flattered and amused by the look she saw in his eyes. Was he aware that there was raw desire there? "You think this is too much skin?"

He took a long sip before he answered, keeping his voice distant, disinterested. "Not if you're a nudist."

"You're a prude, Detective Cavanaugh," she said with a wide grin. "I would have never thought that."

"Just making an observation." He shrugged. "What you wear—or don't wear—is your business."

"Yes, it is," she said congenially, then artfully turned the conversation in another, noncombative direction. "I didn't think you'd show up."

He felt just the slightest bit resentful, as if he were some trained monkey, expected to perform tricks at the behest of the princess.

"I didn't think so, either." Finishing the wine, he

set the empty glass down on a side table. ''But it's a command performance.''

She heard the resentment in his voice. ''I didn't order you to come.''

''I wasn't thinking about you.'' He looked toward his uncle.

She followed his line of vision, then smiled. ''Lovely man, your uncle. Remind me to thank him.'' Before he could say anything in response, she hooked her arm through his. ''Well, now that you're here, let me introduce you around.''

He'd always preferred remaining anonymous. ''Do you have to?''

''Can't tell the players without a score card. Besides, they don't bite.'' An amused expression curved her lips as she cocked her head. ''Do you?''

''I've been known to on occasion.''

''Then I'll steer you clear of Janice Shields,'' she decided out loud, mentioned her older costar, a woman known for her insatiable appetite when it came to good-looking men. ''That'll only excite her.''

He couldn't tell if she was kidding or not, but he saw no reason to doubt her. ''Anyone ever tell you that these people you're around are a little crazy?''

''The word has been bandied about.'' She nodded at a group of people she knew, but decided to hold off with introductions. He'd probably do better on a full stomach. ''I find it helps to be a little crazy in order to stay in this business.''

She was steering him toward the buffet table first. Food he could deal with, he thought. ''Then why stay?''

''Because it's the best game in town.'' Taking a plate, she handed the first to him, then helped herself to another. ''Because I get paid for playing dress-up.'' She took a small serving of the salad, then offered him the ladle. ''And I get to meet fascinating people, like you. What more could I want?''

That was easy. ''Something more normal?'' Bypassing the salad, he went straight to the roast beef.

''Not interested.'' Their eyes met. ''At least, not right now.''

He took that to be fair warning and found himself relaxing just a little, although he wouldn't have been able to explain why.

Chapter Seven

She'd half expected Shaw to duck out of the party when her back was turned. That he didn't both surprised and pleased her. She had to admit that the good-looking police detective corralled her attention more than she thought he should have. But then, most of the men she ran into these days were concerned with the camera getting their best side. Shaw had no such concerns.

Of course, the man did look good from all angles. After this morning, she could sincerely testify to that.

Excusing herself from one of the cast members who had gone on a little too long about getting in touch with her "true self" by being in Aurora, Moira made her way over to the corner that Shaw currently occupied. She noticed that he was sipping what looked to be ginger ale.

"You look like you're in pain. That bad?"

The scent of her perfume, something potent and no doubt expensive as hell, preceded her. Shaw turned to look at her. The party had actually turned out to be better than he'd expected. "As far as evenings go, I've had worse ones."

Joining him, Moira took off her long, dangling earrings and handed them to Shaw. "Hold these for a second, will you?" She massaged her earlobes one at a time. "They always give me a headache."

Shrugging, he slipped them into his pocket. "Then why wear them?"

She winked at him. "We women suffer to look beautiful."

"You don't need earrings for that," he told her. He looked as surprised as she was to hear the words out loud.

"What a lovely thing to say."

"Yeah, well..." Shrugging, not knowing exactly how to respond, he let his voice trail off.

Still massaging, she gave him his reprieve and nodded toward Reese. Again, he was in the center of a bevy of extras slated to play strolling hostesses of the evening in the movie. Each woman was amply endowed. "Your partner looks as if he's having a good time."

Shaw laughed softly to himself. Reese looked as if he'd died and gone to heaven. Twice. "Reese doesn't require much."

She moved ever so slightly so that she could get a better look at his expression. "And you do?"

"Let me rephrase that. Reese likes being around beautiful women."

She cocked her head, studying him. Amused. "And you don't?"

He'd discovered that the most beautiful women were usually consumed with their own looks. He supposed that made her different than the rest. He hadn't seen Moira stop to check out her reflection once all day, not out in the field, not tonight. But then, she seemed to be perfection itself, with amazing staying power. He had a feeling that dirty from the ground on up, she'd still managed to look beautiful.

"That's not my primary requirement, no."

"Then what is?"

"The company of people I like." Which made him wish he were home now, kicking back with his father, or Clay and the girls. Where the clothing of choice was a pair of jeans and a shirt that had been through the spin cycle twelve times too many, instead of a suit that gave him a rash just by existing.

"And you don't like very many people."

"I don't know. I never took a head count." He frowned, draining his glass and looking around for a refill. There was none available. "Look, why are you asking all these questions?"

Moira lifted her shoulders in a casual shrug. "Sorry. It's just the nature of the beast, I guess. I have a tendency to take things apart, dissect them so that I can figure out what makes them tick."

She looked as animated now as she had when she first popped up in his apartment. Didn't the woman ever get tired? He was tired just watching her.

"Wrong word."

"Which one?" She flashed a bright smile at him. "I used a lot of them."

He figured she was fishing for a compliment, but for some reason, he was feeling rather magnanimous at the moment—maybe because he was contemplating his freedom with relish—so he let her have one.

"When you said beast, I take it you were referring to yourself." He moved out of the way as two waiters brought in a huge fresh tray of food. He found himself standing closer to her. "The description hardly applies."

"How would you know?" He saw amusement highlighting her features. "I could be referring to my inner self. Can't tell a book by its cover."

He wondered if she was mocking him, or if he'd just managed to trip over his own tongue. "No, you can't. In case it was unrecognizable, I was trying to give you a compliment."

There was a soft light in her eyes as she looked at him. "Why?" she asked.

It took him a second to drag his own eyes away from her. In this light there was something almost hypnotic about Moira.

"Damned if I know."

"Well, in the name of science and edification, don't you think we should explore this?"

"No." He glanced at his watch. It was late. As it was, he doubted if he'd get right to sleep. Being around her had managed to stimulate him far too much. "I've got to get going."

Taking his wrist, she angled it slightly to look at his watch. She hadn't realized that it was so late. She wanted to be fresh tomorrow so that he'd have no excuse to leave her behind.

"Yeah, me, too." Releasing his wrist, she looked up at him. "Walk me out?"

She looked perfectly capable of walking out on her own. "Everyone in your line of work as pushy as you?"

"I wouldn't know." She saw the second director looking her way. He'd been trying to corner her all night. She knew the moment she was alone he'd pounce on her. As the main star, the movie was riding on her shoulders and she wanted to keep things on a friendly but distant level with the second director.

Moira decided to fudge a little. "I do know that if I start heading for the door alone I'm going to be waylaid by a lot of people who want to get in just one last word. I don't want to be rude, but I do need to get some sleep. If they see me with you, they'll make an assumption and not try to keep me here."

"And what assumption is that?"

She slipped her arm through his and laughed lightly, although he'd said nothing the slightest bit funny. She was doing it, he figured, for her audience.

They began walking toward the exit. "That you and I have another kind of party in mind."

Once outside, she removed her arm from his, freeing him. "Thanks for running interference."

Shaw glanced over his shoulder. He saw Reese looking at him enviously. His partner wasn't the only one watching their exit.

Taking her arm, he walked her toward the elevator. "Why don't I just take you up to your room?" He saw the surprised look that came into her eyes. He didn't want her getting the wrong idea. "In case anyone comes out at the last minute and rides up with you."

He tried to filter out the effects of her smile. "Thank you. I appreciate that."

By the time the elevator car arrived, several people had gathered in the lobby and got on with them. None of them was from the cast party. Shaw noticed that one woman kept looking at Moira, then dropping her glance, not wanting to be guilty of staring.

The last one left in the car got out on the floor below theirs. Just as the woman glanced one last time over her shoulder, Shaw caught her eye and nodded. "Yes, it's her."

The doors closed before the woman could say anything. Moira laughed. He didn't see anything funny about it. "How do you put up with people staring at you?"

She valued her privacy. She valued her hard-won success even more. "I don't mind." The truth was, she enjoyed being famous for the right reasons. "It took a lot of work for me to get to where they *do* stare. It's when they stop staring that I'll worry." The doors opened again, this time on the fifteenth floor. The long corridor was empty. "Well, this is my floor."

Common sense told him to say good-night and ride the car down to the lobby. He didn't follow through. "Might as well do the whole bit," he told Moira as he followed in her wake.

She led the way to her room, her back to him so that Shaw couldn't see her smile. "Your parents raised you well."

"My dad," he corrected.

"Parents divorced?"

"Separated." He thought of the woman who'd been at his father's table last night. His mother. And yet not. What he'd said to Moira was technically true. His parents had been separated, under the oddest of circumstances.

"And your dad raised you." Stopping at her door,

she opened her small clutch purse, looking for her key. "I guess that gives us something in common."

"I guess so," he muttered, trying not to let his thoughts drift too far. They were alone in the hallway. On the floor. And there were things going on inside of him that were best kept in check.

Taking out the card that the desk clerk had issued to her, she pushed it into the slot, then opened the door just the slightest bit. She stuck her heel in as she turned around to face him. "Thank you for being a gentleman and walking me to my door."

He shrugged away her words. She laughed and, one heel still acting as a doorstop, she raised herself slightly on her toes and brushed her lips against his cheek.

The light touch of skin against skin instantly aroused him, placing Shaw on automatic pilot before he quite realized what was happening.

She drew her head back and looked up at him, her eyes staring into his soul. Had he been thinking clearly, he would have taken the opportunity to leave.

But he wasn't.

He didn't.

Instead, he took her into his arms and lowered his mouth to hers as if it had been written somewhere that he should. As if it had been scripted.

The moment he did, he became aware of an excitement spreading through his veins, his limbs, rousing him, bringing his whole body to rigid attention. What he was experiencing was the same kind of rush that coursed through him just before he and Reese raced into a life-and-death scene.

Life and death. Was that the kind of consequences that were awaiting him at the end of this moment?

He didn't know.

He wanted to find out.

Her heart was racing and she felt as if everything inside of her was smiling, a big Cheshire cat–type smile. It wasn't often that she was caught unprepared for the consequences of her actions but this definitely qualified as one of those times.

The man took her breath away. That didn't happen very often; she wouldn't allow it. Despite her carefree attitude, she was very much in control of everything that went on around her. She refused to be someone who allowed things to just happen, refused to simply ride out the waves. She either made them happen or they weren't allowed to touch her life.

This time, it was different. This time, she had no say in what was happening.

It was just happening.

Shaky, feeling like someone who had lived through an earthquake and had no idea of the extent of the damage that had resulted, Moira drew her head back and looked up at the man who had, unintentionally, assaulted her senses as well as her equilibrium.

It took her a second to find enough air to take a

breath. When she did, she blew it out the next moment. "Well, that was a surprise."

"Why?" His glib question, he hoped, hid the fact that he felt about as steady as a cardboard man in the middle of a hurricane. "Didn't you expect me to kiss you?"

Moira took another a deep breath. It did no more to steady her than the last one had. *Logic, talk logic. He likes logic.*

"No, I didn't. I didn't expect you to even walk me to the exit when I asked you."

She had to think he was a complete hick. Shaw banked down the urge to touch her face. "Am I that surly?"

"Independent," she corrected, although the other word fit, too. But right now, she wasn't thinking of him as surly. Another *S* word came to mind. Sexy. Belatedly, she tried to collect herself and smile. "I always find that putting the right spin on things makes them more palatable." Her heart refused to stop pounding. She ran the tip of her tongue over her lips, tasting him. Wanting more. Did he? God, but he was hard to read. "Would you like to come in?"

Yes, he would. But he knew better. "I don't think that would be wise." For either of us, Shaw added silently.

The smile on her lips was small, heartfelt. And hit its target with the force of a silver-tipped arrow scoring a bull's-eye.

"Somehow, I'm not feeling very wise right now, but you're probably right." Subtly, she took another deep breath, trying to steady a pulse that was still scrambling and sending out garbled Morse code to the rest of her body. She offered him what she hoped was a carefree smile. "I'll see you in the morning?"

Shaw nodded, then qualified his response. "At the precinct." He didn't want her popping up at his apartment in the morning. He planned to stop by his father's place tomorrow and he didn't want to bring her along with him. The situation was difficult enough for all concerned as it was without his having to explain things to her. In general, his father was an open man, but until his mother finally came around and remembered them, remembered herself, this definitely fell under the heading of private family business.

He was right, she thought, whether he knew it or not. The way her body tingled right now, just from a simple kiss, being alone with him might not be the wisest thing in the world for her right now.

She nodded. "At the precinct," she repeated.

Moira waited until she saw Shaw walk down the hall and disappear around the corner before she slipped her room card into the slot one more time. Somewhere during that toe-curling kiss, she'd moved forward and allowed her door to lock again.

Pushing the handle down, she opened the door and walked in.

And stopped dead.

Her mouth dropped open. For a second, she felt as if she'd stepped through a time portal into the past.

"What are you doing here?" she asked of the woman sitting on her bed.

"Waiting for you." The other woman pushed aside the magazine she'd been flipping through and smiled.

"How did you get in?"

"I told the man at the desk that I misplaced my card. He couldn't find another one fast enough for me." Her smile widened. "I guess looking like you just keeps paying off."

Moira couldn't believe it. It'd been three years. Three years without a word. And now here Carrie was, in her room, pretending to be her. It was a little difficult to grasp all at once. "Funny, I always thought I looked like you."

Younger by eleven months, her sister was an inch or so taller than she was, and perhaps a little thinner of face, but to the undiscerning eye, they looked enough like one another to be twins. Or, at the very least, pass for each other.

It was a fact that hadn't been wasted on their father. He used their uncanny resemblance whenever he could incorporate it into one of his scams.

The years melted away, as did the hurt at being left to carry on without her. The past was instantly forgiven. What was left was joy, sheer joy at seeing Carrie.

Moira crossed quickly over to the bed, part of her wondering if she was dreaming with her eyes open. Kissing Shaw had addled her brain, so was this a hallucination?

She reached out and took her sister's hand. "What are you doing here?" she asked again. "Why didn't you call, write, send smoke signals, something?"

Carrie shrugged. "I figured it would get lost in the shuffle." Mail addressed to Moira arrived at Firestone Studios in large gray canvas bags by the ton. "Now that you're a big star—"

She didn't want to get into that, didn't want it separating them. She'd been lucky. Carrie had run off with some guy she'd met during their travels. Things hadn't turned out all that well for her.

"Never mind that now. How long can you stay?"

"A while." Carrie pressed her lips together. The look on her face was uncertain, as if she didn't know how to phrase the next part. "That all depends on Simon."

"Simon," Moira repeated. That wasn't the name of the man Carrie had run off with. That had been a Lewis Sotherland. "Who's Simon?"

Carrie took a deep breath. To Moira's way of thinking the smile on her face seemed a little forced. "The man I'm going to marry."

"Marry?" Moira stared hard, searching for the customary joy that traditionally accompanied that kind of declaration. She didn't see it. What was going on here? ''My God, you just drop out of the sky after three years and tell me I'm going to have a brother-in-law? Wow.''

Trying to be thrilled for her, Moira hugged her sister. She felt Carrie wince against her, heard the whimper that escaped before she could press her lips together.

Moira drew back, wary. Worried. And suspicious. ''What's the matter? I haven't gotten that strong, or you that weak,'' she added.

Carrie looked away, unable to meet her eyes. ''Nothing.''

Puzzled, concerned, Moira deliberately pressed her fingers against the left side of her sister's rib cage. Carrie winced even as she pulled away. Moira matched her movement for movement, peering at her face, trying to read between the lines.

''Carrie?''

Carrie deliberately avoided looking at her. ''It's nothing.''

The hell it was. ''Let me see 'nothing.'''

Her sister began to back away, but Moira grabbed hold of her blouse and managed to pull it up before Carrie could step back. There, pressed against her flesh, was an ugly rainbow of colors—yellow, blue, green with a dash of purple—swirling around in an uneven swatch. Moira's heart froze. Her voice was stony as she raised her eyes to her sister's face. ''How did you get that?''

Before Carrie could answer, Moira heard the

sound of the toilet being flushed. The realization that there was someone else in the hotel room with them penetrated just as the bathroom door opened and a tall, dark-haired handsome man walked out. A broad smile graced his tanned face. Moira caught herself thinking that whoever this was, he looked like a matinee idol and had the swagger to match.

Carrie took the opportunity to snatch back the edge of her blouse and tuck it back into her jeans.

The man extended his hand toward her as he approached. ''Hi. You must be Moira. And I'm—''

She'd noted the way her sister shrank into herself when she first turned to look at the man. It was probably all unconscious, Moira thought, and all the more telling because of it.

Her expression was unsmiling. ''The man who gave my sister that bruise?''

Simon looked taken aback by the accusation. ''What?'' The look he tossed Carrie was just the slightest bit accusing. ''Hell, no. She walks into things a lot—don't you, Carrie?''

Carrie's head bobbed on cue. ''Uh-huh, all the time.'' She flashed a weak smile at her sister. ''You know how I was.''

Moira's eyes were steely. It took everything she had not to fling herself at the man, her nails extended. Ever since her mother had died, she'd been the matriarch, the protective one. Feelings like that didn't fade away over time.

''Yes, I do. Dad used to call you the steady one.''

Carrie nervously ran her tongue along her lips. She made Moira think of a skittish animal waiting for the jaws of a trap to snap shut.

"I'm older now," her sister told her. "I got clumsy."

Moira's eyes narrowed. What had he done to her carefree sister? "Only in your choice of men."

"Hey, you have no call to say that." Simon took a step closer to her, anger flashing in his dark eyes.

Aligning herself with Carrie, Moira indicated the door. "I'd like you to leave please."

Simon remained where he was. He looked at Carrie accusingly. "You didn't tell me your sister was a bitch. C'mon, Carrie."

Moira moved to block her sister's way, her eyes on the man. "No, not her. Just you."

He reached for Carrie's hand, but Moira stopped him. "She goes where I tell her to go."

"Not anymore."

His expression turned malevolent. "And who's going to stop her? You? You won't look so pretty with your face rearranged."

"Simon—" Carrie protested, panicked.

"Shut up, Carrie."

Moira raised her chin pugnaciously. "Neither will you behind bars. Not after a while. Pretty men like you are considered fresh meat there. You lay one finger on me—or my sister—and you're going to have to kill me because I'll be calling the police the second I scrape myself off the floor. Now get out of here,'' she ordered, ''before I call security.''

''You women are all alike,'' he growled.

''No,'' she said, her eyes shooting daggers at him. ''We're not.''

Simon managed to grab Carrie's wrist. ''You're coming with me.''

Carrie began to struggle. Moira grabbed his hand and began peeling his fingers away from Carrie's wrist.

''Let go of her!'' she shouted.

The next second, Moira heard someone knocking loudly on the door. ''Moira, are you all right?''

Her heart leaped into her throat. It was Shaw.

Chapter Eight

Moving Simon aside, Moira lost no time in getting to the door and throwing it open.

Shaw glimpsed what looked like relief on Moira's face as she stepped back to admit him. There were two other people inside the room. Well-honed instincts instantly kicked in. Shaw took one look at the man and knew this was no late-evening tryst he'd walked in on.

He could feel the tension in the room. His eyes shifted back to Moira. "Anything wrong?"

She could have hugged him. While she never doubted that she could handle Simon, that the man who badgered her sister around was at bottom a coward the way all abusers were, it was nice to have backup.

"Not anymore," she told Shaw. She looked at Simon. "This man was just leaving, weren't you?"

Anger smoldered in Simon's eyes as he looked at Carrie. Whatever he'd hoped for by coming here with her sister—and Moira could make a better-than-educated guess as to what that was—it was not panning out for him. Given half a chance, she knew he would take his frustration out on Carrie. "You coming?" Simon asked.

Moira placed herself between Simon and her sister. "No, I already told you, she's not. She's staying here with me." She slipped her arm around her sister's shoulders. The protective gesture was not lost on Shaw. "We have a lot of catching up to do."

The man looked as if he might be debating making a stand after all. Shaw shifted his weight, issuing a silent warning to him. "The lady said leave."

If looks could kill, there would have been three dead bodies within the room. "The lady hasn't heard the last of this yet," Simon warned before storming out of the suite and slamming the door behind him.

Moira blew out a sigh of relief, then flashed an encouraging smile at the woman beside her.

Shaw's eyes shifted from one woman to the other. They looked alike. Not so he would mistake one for the other when they were standing side by side. Seeing them both, he could readily identify which one was Moira. But he wasn't so sure about his ability to tell one from the other if he'd happened along just one of them.

Moira's eyes were greener, he decided. And she looked a lot more in control, more vivid than the woman next to her.

Shaw made the natural assumption. "Is this your sister?"

"My baby sister," Moira qualified with the kind of warm pride that had no foundations other than love.

The woman flushed. "Eleven months. Moira's just eleven months older." Belatedly, she put out her hand. "My name's Carrie."

Moira snorted. "Your name would have been mud if you had gone with him."

She shook her head, still stunned that the vibrant, gregarious sister she'd once known would have allowed herself to become subjugated by a man like that. Granted, Simon was good-looking, but looks only went so far. Kindness could bridge all sorts of gaps, and if she was any judge of character, she knew that the man her sister was involved with didn't have a drop of kindness in him.

Carrie shrugged nervously. "He'll cool off. He'll be fine."

"He'll be alone," Moira insisted. She saw the look on Carrie's face. Given half a chance, she'd forgive the man who had abused her and go back to him. She could hardly believe it, but there it was, in Carrie's eyes. "I don't want you seeing him again."

The moment threatened to erupt in a confrontation between the sisters.

"So she's bossy like that with everyone?" Shaw asked the other woman, seeking to lighten the tension, at least while he was still in the room.

Carrie nodded. "Pretty much." Her smile faded a little as she looked at Moira. "It's one of the reasons I left."

"And maybe one of the reasons you came back," Moira guessed.

But this was something that needed discussing later, privately. Moira looked at Shaw. Under other circumstances, his appearance on her doorstep might have been the beginning of something. But not right now. Not while she had Carrie to worry about.

"Speaking of coming back, why did you?" She wasn't going to allow herself to speculate about the reasons for his return. "Not that I'm not grateful for the cavalry appearing at just the right moment," she added.

"You forgot these." Slipping his hand into his right pocket, Shaw took out the earrings she'd handed him in the ballroom. He held them up. They caught the light and flirted with it. "I thought you might want them."

Moira saw her sister's eyes grow huge as she looked at the dangling earrings. If they'd been real, they would have easily been worth twenty thousand dollars—each. "Thanks." She took them from Shaw. "But you didn't have to come back for that."

He shrugged. "I didn't like the idea of carrying around expensive jewelry in my pocket."

"You weren't." When he raised an inquiring eyebrow, she explained, "This is just costume jewelry."

He laughed shortly. They certainly had fooled him. And given him a reason to return, which had turned out fortunate for everyone. He's seen people like that guy before. They got off by threatening women.

Shaw touched the tip of one earring in her palm. "Sure looks real."

"That's the thing about fakes." Moving over to the bureau, she deposited the earrings. "In the right setting, they can fool you." She looked deliberately at her sister. But Carrie seemed oblivious to her meaning.

Shaw glanced toward the door. He wasn't sure how the other man fit into all this, but he hadn't liked the looks of him.

"Do you want me to stick around for a while?" he offered.

Yes, Moira thought, she did. But not for the reason he surmised. Besides, she needed to have a long talk with her sister. That couldn't happen if Shaw remained.

She hooked her arm through his and walked the

short distance to the door. The smile she flashed didn't show the reluctance she was experiencing.

"No, that's all right. I don't think he'll come back. Cowards rarely do."

"Cowards have a way of lashing out when you least expect it. They go for the soft underbelly," Shaw said.

Moira grinned, patting her flat stomach. "My underbelly is hard."

He sincerely doubted that. What was worse, he felt an urge to make the determination himself. Maybe he had better hit the trail after all. "I'll see you tomorrow."

She stood holding the door open for a moment. "Count on it."

And in an odd sort of way that didn't altogether please him, he did count on it.

The moment she closed the door, Moira turned around to look at Carrie. The pep talk she was going to launch into faded. Tears shimmered in her sister's eyes. Tears always reduced her to mush, especially Carrie's tears. Moira took her hand and led her sister over to the bed. Sitting down on the edge, she put her arm around Carrie's slender shoulders and just held her to her for a few seconds.

"I'm glad you're here, Carrie-Bear," she said quietly, using the nickname she hadn't uttered since they were both children. It was the nickname their mother had given Carrie. "I've missed you."

Carrie sighed, trying to hold back a sob, battling

a hundred demons. Gravitating toward one. "Moira, I love him."

She knew Carrie did—that was what made all of this so hard. Moira hated the man she hardly knew, hated him for ever hurting someone she loved, and she loved her sister fiercely. Moira paused, searching for the right words to soften this, knowing there weren't any. "I don't think he loves you."

Carrie's head jerked up. Anger mingled with pain in her eyes. "How can you say that?"

She thought of the bruise she'd see on Carrie's rib cage. Thought of it and knew that it hadn't been the first. Wouldn't be the last if she let Carrie go back to him. Like as not, the man would take out on her what had happened here.

"Because," she began patiently, "you don't hit the person you love."

Carrie rose and began to pace around the room. "So, he has a temper. Lots of people have tempers."

Was Carrie so blind, or was the view just better from a distance? "He has a *problem* and I don't want you to be part of it."

Carrie became defensive, fighting battles for Simon that he couldn't fight on his own. "He doesn't mean it."

That was an old, familiar refrain. Moira had heard enough stories to know what usually followed. Remorse, promises and more and more serious beatings.

"None of them mean it. It's a sickness, Carrie,

but it's a sickness that has casualties and I don't want you to be one of them."

She watched Carrie pace about the room. Same old Carrie. Any second now, she was going to work up a head of steam and leave. Moira couldn't let that happen.

Ever practical, Moira's mind turned toward details. "Do you live around here?"

Carrie shook her head. "We move around."

And didn't that have a familiar ring? Moira mused. After their mother died, they'd moved around so much that at one point, she was convinced they were nomads or gypsies. But this was Carrie and she didn't want to scare her off. She didn't press for details. Carrie would tell her in her own good time.

The first thing was to make her sister feel secure. "Good. Then I won't be uprooting you." She tried to look as innocent as possible. Carrie had always been her toughest audience. "How would you like to do me a favor?"

Carrie looked at her, her expression puzzled. "*You* need a favor?"

Moira had a feeling that her sister thought she had everything. In a manner of speaking, she did. What she had was glamour and money. But there were other things that were sorely missing, things money couldn't begin to buy.

"I need a stand-in," she told Carrie glibly, then grew more serious. "More than that, I need family."

Her smile was meant to break down walls. ''What do you say? Want the job?''

A smile played on Carrie's lips, reflecting relief. ''What'll I have to do to qualify?''

Moira laughed, relieved as she hugged her. That had been a great deal less painless than she'd anticipated. ''Just be you.''

''How's your sister doing?'' Shaw asked Moira as he walked into the squad room the next morning, trying to bank down the feeling that he'd been looking forward to seeing her all morning.

He'd given breakfast and the woman who was the center of it—his mother—his full attention. Even so, his thoughts kept drifting back to last night. To the relief on Moira's face when he'd shown up. To the way her eyes had fluttered shut when he'd kissed her in the hall. To the way her lips had felt against his. No matter how hard he tried, he couldn't shake free of the thoughts about her.

She was dressed much the way she'd been dressed yesterday morning—jeans, a shirt, shoes that allowed her to move fast if she had to. None of which were nearly as breath-stealing as the outfit she'd had on last night.

But he had come armed with his imagination, and that was both good and bad.

Moira set down the near-empty container of coffee on his desk. ''Better. Thanks for asking.'' And then she grinned. ''I now have a stand-in.''

He was getting to like her grin. To wait for it. Which wasn't good. "Excuse me?"

"A stand-in. Someone who takes my place while they check the lighting, block the scene, things like that."

"You gave her a job?" He would have expected her to give her sister money, if anything. Maybe she wasn't quite as much of an airhead as he'd originally thought.

"I gave her a way out," she corrected. "You know, give a man a fish, you feed him for a day, teach him to fish—"

"And he's stuck cleaning fish for the rest of his life." He saw the look on her face. "My dad used to take us fishing. I never seemed to catch anything so I got cleaning detail." Then, in case she thought he was being critical, he added, "What you did was a good thing."

Moira pressed her lips together. "Simon was using her as a punching bag."

The policeman within him pushed to the foreground. "She want to press charges?"

She shook her head. "I'm lucky I got her to stay with me instead of him." This was Carrie's life and she had no business discussing it, even if she was worried about her sister. Moira saw Reese walking toward them and waved to the man. She glanced in Shaw's direction. "Are we ready to roll?"

He laughed. "Yeah, we're ready to roll."

The day, he thought as he walked to meet his partner, promised to be an interesting one.

It broke her heart.

The kind of life she and her father and sister had led never took them to the seamier streets, the kind she found herself on now as Reese and Shaw drove around, looking for underage prostitutes to question. It wasn't easy. Word had gotten around and the girls were scattering like so many mice before a hungry cat.

Her father, Moira realized as she looked around, had sheltered them from this kind of thing. Sheltered them from the despair, the poverty that first ate away at a person's self-respect, then devoured all hope, leaving nothing but a skeleton of misery in its place.

She wished she knew where her father was now, so she could thank him. The kind of life they'd led hadn't been orthodox, but he'd done what he could to make sure they had what they needed.

Moira saw despair on the faces of the women who paraded themselves on the corner.

She rocked back and forth on her seat, impatient. Captive of her word. She'd given it to Shaw, saying she was going to stay inside the car the way he'd told her to. It allowed her only the vaguest of views. But even that was almost too much.

Old before their time, worn-out, these women who sold their bodies in order to survive another day were the walking dead. It was only a matter of time before they turned up as lifeless corpses, victims of some kind of terrible crime.

Moira shivered as she watched Shaw approach yet another prostitute. How could he stand going out into this day after day? How did he keep from having it drain him dry? Did he reconnect with something life-affirming every night? Was that what kept him going? She didn't know, but she was certainly beginning to admire the man a great deal.

They'd been at this the better part of the day, riding around to corners like this one, questioning the women they did find, searching for the younger ones, the dropouts and the runaways who had no idea what they were getting themselves into.

Jenkins, the porno shop owner, had given them the name of his landlord, the man who held both the deed to the firetrap that housed his business and who'd supplied the Kiddies for Kicks tapes that had been found on the premises. But as of this morning, the landlord was nowhere to be found. Shaw had a hunch that he would turn up in some shallow grave somewhere. This was bigger than just some lowly scum.

They needed more leads. If enough leads came their way, one of them would hopefully send them off into the right direction.

All it took was one.

Moira continued staring out the window, wishing she was closer, wishing she could hear what was being said, but Shaw had been very stern as he'd issued his warning. He'd underscored it by saying he didn't want her in harm's way. It was either his way or no way and she had a feeling that this time, he meant it.

The man was accustomed to being obeyed, she thought absently. She watched him approach a young girl. At first, she thought the girl had just lost her way and wandered into this part of town by accident. She looked so incredibly young.

But then she took a closer look. The girl had already assumed the uniform of the trade. A short, vinyl skirt, boots that covered far more of her than her clothing did and enough makeup to outfit a busy cosmetic counter at any major department store.

Moira couldn't turn her eyes away.

Damn it, what was she, fourteen? Fifteen? The girl should have been home, daydreaming about the latest boy band, not looking around for someone to throw her a few dollars for the use of her body.

She saw Shaw giving the girl money. For information?

Without thinking, Moira got out of the car and headed straight for them.

Reese saw her coming first. "Uh-oh. Torpedo at nine o'clock."

Shaw glared at his partner, not bothering to hide his annoyance. This was the first underage prostitute they'd managed to come across and he didn't want anything scaring her away. Like her sisters of the trade, the girl was uncooperative, but he had a feeling that he could get her to come around if he only pressed the right buttons. He'd given her a hundred dollars, not for information, but for a respite. If he gave it to her, that meant she didn't have to sell herself for the amount.

"What the hell are you talking about?"

"Our ride-along," Reese managed to say before Moira was there next to them.

She couldn't keep her eyes off the girl. Close up, the makeup was even more appalling. A pathetic child playing dress-up in a macabre world.

"How old are you?" Moira demanded.

"Moira, get back into the car or I swear I'll send you back to your studio in a box," Shaw barked.

"Moira?" the girl repeated, clearly impressed despite the bored, woman-of-the-world stance she was so desperately attempting to emulate.

"Moira McCormick," she introduced herself. "And I'm not the issue here. How old are you?"

"Eighteen." The lie was automatic and laughable. She looked thunderstruck. "Moira McCormick, the movie star?"

Looking at her, Shaw could almost see the gears in Moira's head shifting. "Yes. Do you want a job?"

"What?" The incredulous question had come from Shaw as Reese looked on, as dumbstruck as his partner.

Moira ignored the two men, her attention completely focused on the girl. On saving the girl.

"I'm making a movie here in Aurora. I need extras. You've got the right face for it—with a little less makeup. The pay's three hundred dollars a day. And hot food," she added. From the looks of the girl, meals had not been all that plentiful.

The girl looked torn between being skeptical and elated. "Who do I have to do?"

"Nobody," Moira said firmly.

He'd had enough. Shaw grabbed Moira firmly by the arm and dragged her aside. "What the hell do you think you're doing?"

"Offering her a way out." How callous had his heart gotten while he worked these streets? "She's a baby."

"She could also be the key to unlocking everything. So that 'babies' like her aren't bought and sold—and who knows what else—for some creep's sick pleasure."

"She can be a 'key' working at a different profession, can't she? It doesn't change what she knows, what she can tell you. And maybe if she's not scared, not surrounded by this kind of filth, she will tell you what you want to know." She struggled against the tide of emotion welling up within her. "Shaw, look at her. That's someone's daughter."

He knew that. And he was trying to save a lot of people's daughters, not just one. But, he supposed, as surprising as it was, Moira was making sense. He thought of what she'd told him this morning, about giving her sister a job. Apparently her do-goodism wasn't restricted to just family. "And what are you, Saint Moira?"

"No. Just doing my part whenever I can."

He was beginning to believe she meant that. And she did have a point. If the girl wasn't in this element, she might not be afraid of any reprisals and would talk to them. Looking over her head, his eyes met Reese's and he nodded.

"Okay—" he took her arm again "—go, do your part. It might even help."

The girl stood watching her, wary, afraid. Awestruck. "Did you mean it?" she asked the moment Moira approached her. "What you said about the work?"

"Absolutely." And if there wasn't some small part for her in the script, she'd have the writer create one. "What's your name?"

"Desiree."

She looked at the girl. "What's your real name?"

The girl looked down at the ground, as if she was debating how far she could trust this woman she knew only through the magic of Hollywood. And then she looked up again. "Amy. Amy Kendell."

"Well, Amy Kendell—" she smiled warmly at the girl "—it's nice to meet you." Moira fished out a card from her pocket. "Here's my card." She took the pencil Shaw had been using to make notes and wrote on the back of the card. "And here's the name and number of the casting director. Ralph Ebersole." She said the name slowly, letting it sink in.

"Tell him that Moira McCormick sent you and if he has any questions, to call me." She gave Amy the card. "Now do me a favor."

The girl eyed her with a wariness that seemed embedded in her. "Yeah?"

"Get off this street corner. Go home and take a shower. Watch a little TV. And then call Ralph. Remind him that he still owes me a favor and I'm calling him on it."

Shaw remained with the girl a few more minutes, telling her to get in contact with them the moment her "memory" about things returned.

He had a feeling that they had found one of the girls that was being used in the underage prostitution ring. Only sitting down and viewing the scores of tapes they had seized from Jenkins's porno shop would tell him whether or not he was right. The idea of the task sickened him, but someone had to do it.

Moira, he thought, walking back to the squad car, looking at her very pleased face, might very well have allowed them to get their first decent lead.

Chapter Nine

Andrew hadn't thought it would be this hard on him. All these years of looking for some trace of Rose, for some clue that verified that she was still alive, he'd thought that the search was the most difficult part. That once he'd found her, everything that came afterward would take on a positive glow.

But watching her interact with him and their children, politely but with a built-in reserve whose origin he couldn't begin to guess at, was proving to be even more difficult for him than enduring the constant uncertainty that had been the cornerstone of all the years of searching. It threatened to rip his heart out, not once but several times over.

She was with him and yet she wasn't.

"I feel like Jimmy Stewart in *Vertigo,* trying to make Kim Novak over into the woman I lost just because she looked like her," he'd confided to Shaw this morning just before his oldest left the house.

Shaw had come for breakfast, joining a full complement at the table. Even some of their cousins had shown up to lend support. During the meal, conversation had moved along, but not with the flow it usually had. It was as if they were all still holding their collective breath.

"Except that we're sure this is Mom," Shaw had been quick to point out. "The fingerprints proved it. You're not trying to make her over, Dad. You're trying to help her remember. It takes time."

He'd nodded, looking at the woman he loved with all his heart talking to one of their daughters. It would have taken such a little stretch for everything to be all right. "Yes, it does," he'd agreed. "At least I know that she's alive, that she's safe. That's a hell of a lot more than I knew for the past fifteen years."

He'd looked at his oldest, grateful that Shaw had managed to swing by. Grateful for the entire support system that was in place and always had been, ever since the beginning. That was all to Rose's credit, not his. She'd raised them while he'd been out, making their corner of the world safe, forgetting at times that his first allegiance should have been to his own.

But Rose hadn't. She'd kept the home fires burning, kept their kids on the right track by putting them on the path that eventually led them to becoming the fine men and women they were today. All Rose's doing, and she didn't remember any of it, he thought now sadly.

He'd squeezed his older son's shoulder. "Thanks for coming."

Shaw had shifted his weight slightly. Gratitude, Andrew knew, was something his oldest wasn't comfortable with. Shaw had never liked praise. "We're all here for you, Dad."

Andrew knew that to be true. Knew, too, that he shouldn't be impatient, shouldn't allow this temporary standstill to wound him as much as it did. He reminded himself that if Rose had been in possession of her memory all these long years, she would have returned to him, to them, on her own long ago.

Something had happened to her to blank out her memory of who and what she was. He was grateful that the circumstances had arranged themselves so that he could find her. That last gap, the one that led her back to the family who loved her, would be crossed, too, he promised himself. In good time.

Now, with the last of their children leaving, Andrew rose from the table, gathering up his own plate. He always ate last, after he was sure everyone else had their fill.

He could feel her looking at him. What was she thinking? She'd been here for several days. Was anything the slightest bit familiar to her?

"I'm sorry."

He stopped and wearily set down his plate on the table. "You don't have to keep saying that."

"I know. But I am." She smiled bravely at him, but there was no love behind the expression, no secret communication. She was still Claire and not Rose. "I just can't remember. I thought that if I came here, if I met them, if I stayed in the house where you said we lived—" He hated the way she qualified that, but he held his tongue. In her place, he might have felt the same way. Wary, uncertain. "—I would remember. But I don't." She sighed and shook her head, dragging her fingers through her hair just the way she used to do. Just the way her daughters did now. "I feel I should know you, know all of you." Her smile was brave and apologetic. "If I did, it would be a lovely thing because you all seem like such nice people—"

"You made us that way," he interrupted.

She didn't see how that was possible. He was just being kind. How many years had she dreamed about someone like him? Someone kind and good? The entire time she'd lived near Bainbridge-by-the-sea. "According to you, I've been gone fifteen years."

Because he knew the way her mind worked even if she didn't, he knew what she was going to say. "But you laid the foundation. Took care of the kids. Gave me someone I loved to come home to."

Claire smiled sadly. Reaching out, she touched his

face, gliding her fingertips lightly along his cheek. Wishing with all her heart that the blindfold would finally lift from her mind. But it was secure, refusing to let more than the smallest glimmer, the tiniest inkling that something was vaguely familiar, in. It frustrated her more than words could say.

"I wish..." Claire began, then her voice trailed off.

He turned her palm in toward his lips and kissed it lightly. The way someone who'd spent a lifetime with a mate would. He saw something fleeting in her eyes, but it was gone before he could grasp it.

"I know." And then there was something else in her eyes. A restlessness that made him nervous. Did she want to go? She couldn't leave—not now, not yet. Not until she remembered. He struggled to curb his own fears. "Give it time."

"Time," Claire echoed. That was all she'd ever had. Time and an uneasiness that haunted her dreams like a specter without a face.

She rose from the table, a need to be busy taking precedence over everything else. She needed to feel useful, to work, not vegetate like some specimen in a laboratory petri dish.

"Let me handle those," she told him, moving Andrew aside. She began to pick up the breakfast dishes, stacking them on top of one another. "At least it's something I know."

"There'll be more, I promise." Dishes in her

hands, she looked at him then, as if afraid to believe him. "I never break a promise," he told her.

Claire merely nodded and continued stacking the plates together.

Aiming the remote control at the twenty-inch television set the department kept inside the smaller of the two conference rooms on the floor, Shaw terminated the hazy image on the screen in front of him.

He felt utterly drained and in silent despair for the human race. If it could spawn creatures who took pleasure in what he'd just been subjected to, then maybe the human race really wasn't worth saving. Maybe it wasn't worth putting his life on the line every day.

He needed a stiff drink. Something to anesthetize his brain and make him forget all this.

Shaw closed his eyes, waiting for the tension to leave his shoulders, his body. So far he hadn't found the girl Moira had befriended the other day. When he'd questioned her, Amy had turned out to know very little. Or so she maintained. What she did tell him was that she'd heard the so-called studio where these videos were made was completely mobile. That was borne out by the tapes he'd already watched. The movies were filmed anywhere and everywhere—the inside of a van, different motel rooms, attics, basements, any place that allowed a smattering of light in. Always with girls who looked as if they belonged in high school if not middle school.

It made his flesh creep and his stomach turn. He would have liked to toss aside his gun and badge and spend ten minutes alone with the so-called film-makers. It wouldn't have accomplished anything, but it would have made him feel better.

Shaw squinted as the door opened. Fluorescent light from the precinct hallway pooled into the room. A hazy halo glowed around the woman in the doorway. For a second, he couldn't make out who it was.

The next moment, he knew.

She didn't have to say a word. He didn't even have to see her. Her perfume, distinct, evocative, preceded her. He took a deep breath, wishing the scent could erase what he'd just viewed. But it couldn't. He doubted that anything could.

Moira took a step into the room, peering at his face. There was concern on hers. "Are you all right?"

"Sure," he snapped a little too quickly, then caught himself. "Why shouldn't I be?"

Moira slipped her hands into her pockets. "Well, for one thing, you look as if you could bite the head off a live chicken. For another, you've been in here for a while."

She glanced at her watch. He'd barred her from the room, not that she would have wanted to watch what he was viewing. That had been over three hours ago. She'd spent the time with Reese and moving around the floor, talking to various police officers. But all the while, her mind had been on Shaw and what he was doing.

She gave him her warmest, most sympathetic smile. "I thought that maybe you were entitled for some time off for good behavior."

She talked as if she understood what he was going through. As if she knew how disgusted all this made him feel. But how could she know? She came from the world of make-believe and he came from a world where reality arrived outfitted with razor-sharp spikes that could eat into your flesh.

Shaw pushed back his chair and rose to his feet, tossing the remote onto the table in front of him. "Yeah, I think I'll call it a night."

He sounded weary, she thought, and tense. She made her own diagnosis. "Reese is taking me to the Shannon. Would you like to come?"

"The Shannon?" Shaw echoed. She was talking about the local bar where they all hung out after work. It was strictly a cop bar and outsiders were not encouraged. Knowing that his partner probably wanted to impress her, he would have thought Reese would want to take her to a high-end restaurant. "Why is he taking you there?"

"Atmosphere," she explained. "The Shannon is part of your life, isn't it?" She didn't wait for him to answer. "I'm thinking of asking Joshua to put in a scene in the movie using a local hangout."

He looked at her blankly. "Joshua?"

"Walhberg." She gave him the famous screenwriter's last name and saw that it meant as much to Shaw as the first name had. Zero. "He's the one who wrote the script."

Shaw laughed shortly, popping the tape out of the VCR and putting it on top of the viewed pile. "You get to boss him around, too?"

"It'll be strictly a suggestion," she informed him. "The rest will be up to Joshua. But I think a scene like that might make my character seem more human to the audience."

He tried to follow her reasoning. "And going to a bar makes me more human?"

She didn't know about that, but she did know one thing. Moira nodded at the pile of tapes beside the VCR. There were dozens more in the boxes on the floor. "Watching that kind of filth and not going on a rampage makes you a saint. I figure maybe you wanted to counterbalance that."

"A saint." Reese laughed, coming into the conference room to join them. Reaching over on the wall, he flipped on the light switch. "Now there's something nobody ever accused Cavanaugh of being." Becoming serious, he nodded toward the dormant television set. "You find her yet? Amy." He said the girl's name in case Shaw didn't know to whom he was referring.

"No."

So far, Amy had only said she knew of the tapes,

and of girls she'd told them had been snatched up off the street and forced to make these videos. But she'd sworn that she hadn't been one of them. Whether that was the truth or not still remained to be seen.

Moira looked from one man to the other. After a long session at the police station, Amy had come back to the hotel with her last night. She'd gotten the girl a room across the floor from her own. "Would you like me to talk to her?"

Shaw paused to consider the offer. The woman was a born orchestrator, not to mention meddler, but this time it appeared to be doing some good.

"Maybe that's not a bad idea," Shaw allowed. Since she was determined to be part of this, he might as well use her where she did the most good. "Seeing as how you've got her staying at a room in the hotel."

As far as he knew, Moira was paying for that out of her own pocket, and while the actress could well afford it, it wasn't something he figured most people did for total strangers. He had to grudgingly admit that Moira McCormick was a unique woman.

Moira wondered if she had finally won him over. She had strong reservations about that. Shaw was not easily led, like the rest of them. She recalled her father's advice on the subject. *Always play up to the hardest mark in the room. You win him over, you've got everyone in the palm of your hand.* She was willing to bet that right now, she had everyone *but* Shaw in the palm of her hand.

She nodded. "I'll see if I can get Amy to trust me."

He laughed shortly as he walked out of the room behind Moira and Reese. "Why not? You seem to have everyone else eating out of your hand."

Funny that he should use the exact same image she'd just thought of. She looked at Reese, knowing she could count on Shaw's partner for support.

"Is it just me, or did he sound as if he was accusing me of something?"

Reese shrugged good-naturedly. "That's just Cavanaugh's way. He's not happy unless he's grumpy."

Moira pretended to consider that as she stopped and cocked her head to look at Shaw. "Isn't that a contradiction in terms?"

"Yeah, but so's Cavanaugh."

"Hey—" Shaw tapped Reese on the shoulder "—I'm right here, remember?"

In silent agreement, they all headed toward the elevator together.

"Yeah, I know," Reese lamented. "You wouldn't be except that Moira insisted we bring you along. Thought you might need to reconnect with the human race." The elevator arrived and Reese waited for Moira to get in first before he followed her. "I told her that it was an impossible cause, but she seems to think you can be redeemed."

Shaw said nothing as he got in behind them. After viewing the tapes, he was more inclined to agree with Reese than Moira.

She held court at the Shannon pretty much the way she had that first day at the precinct. The same way, he had no doubt, she probably did at the movie studio. He sat at the bar with Reese, pretending he wasn't watching her. Unable to help watching her. People just seemed to gravitate toward her, women as well as men. Like bees to honey. It wasn't just her looks, or that she was a celebrity. Moira seemed to be able to pull people in by the sheer magnetism of her outgoing personality.

Shaw stared into the bottom of his mug. It occurred to him that it was the fourth or so one he had since he'd come into the establishment. How had that happened? Looking to his left, he saw that the spot was empty. Attempting to focus his thoughts, he vaguely remembered that Reese had excused himself, saying there was someone he wanted to talk to. One of the uniformed women, wasn't it?

When was that? He couldn't remember.

It had been a hell of a day and it appeared that he was on his way to forgetting it. Just as well.

"So, what's it like, having her riding around with you?"

Shaw looked to his left. The space was no longer empty. A patrolman sat in the seat that had belonged to Reese. His question rang of eagerness; his eyes were shining as he turned to look at Moira.

Shaw debated ordering another beer, then decided against it. Maybe he'd stop at the liquor store on his way home to complete the job he'd begun here. There were still viable parts of his brain that could think. That could remember the way he'd spent his afternoon.

He realized that the officer at his elbow waited for an answer.

''It's a royal pain in the butt,'' Shaw finally responded. Digging into his pocket, he took out a few dollars and left them on the counter as a tip. He had to get going while he could still function. ''She doesn't stop talking, asking endless questions.'' He remembered the first day, when she'd used the car as a roadblock. ''Won't listen when I tell her to stay put.''

The officer bobbed his head up and down, absorbing every word as if it were pure gold. It was easy to see, even through his slightly unfocused eyes, that the other man was more than a little smitten with the actress.

''Have you had any time alone with her?'' the patrolman asked, turning to look at him. He leaned his head in, as if that somehow made the words secretive. ''You know what I mean.''

Shaw's brain cleared a little. He thought of the kiss at her hotel door. Even thinking about it generated a sweet, tempting warmth that coursed over his body, reminding him that celibacy was highly overrated and he was overdue to leave its ranks.

But not with her, he told himself.

"No," Shaw said firmly.

"If it was me..." The officer didn't have to finish. The leer on his face, in his voice, said it all.

Shaw had no idea why, but he took offense for Moira. Or maybe it was the beer talking, stirring something akin of jealousy within him, sending it streaming through his veins.

The very idea was ridiculous, but he couldn't seem to shake free of its effects. His voice was low, dangerous. "But it's not you, is it?"

The officer took one look at Shaw's face, picked up his mug and retreated.

The next moment, Reese was back, filling the seat and the space. A fresh mug of ale was in his hand and he lifted it in Moira's direction. "She blends in and stands out at the same time, doesn't she?"

Shaw blew out a breath. "What are you, her publicity agent suddenly?"

"No, just a young man in love." Reese pretended to sigh, then laughed as he looked at him. "Don't worry. I'm not treading on your territory. I've just made some very impressive arrangements of my own to spend the rest of the evening with Officer Rhonda. Mind if I keep the car?" he asked, referring to the fact that he had been the one to drive the vehicle here.

Shaw scowled, waving away the question. "Go

ahead, knock yourself out.'' The next moment, the rest of Reese's statement replayed itself in his brain. ''What the hell are you talking about?'' If his partner was insinuating there was something going on between him and the actress, Reese was in a far more inebriated state than he was. ''There's nothing going on between us. There *is* no territory.''

Reese hid his smile behind the mug. ''She might have other ideas.'' He raised his eyes to his partner's stony face. ''So would you if you let yourself be something other than Supercop for a while.''

Shaw could only shake his head. ''As your friend, I'm advising you to stop drinking now. It's affecting your judgment.''

Reese took another sip, then put down the mug. ''What's your excuse?''

Maybe he *had* had too much to drink. Nothing Reese was saying was making any sense to him. ''For what?''

''For having lousy judgment.''

Shaw waved a dismissive hand at his partner and got up off the bar stool. He'd had enough of inane conversation. It was time to go. He was vaguely aware of saying something in parting to Reese, but for the life of him, he wasn't sure just what. Just as well, the man was probably too enamored with Moira to think or hear clearly.

Not like him.

Damn, but he felt as if his emotions were all over the place right now. Things like feelings just got in the way of doing a good job. But now, with his father going through hell, his mother making a reappearance in their lives after so many years and not knowing any of them, damn, it was enough to push any man over the brink.

And that was without having to play nursemaid to a Hollywood celebrity. Someone should give him a medal, he thought.

Shaw made it to the door before he became aware that there was anyone behind him. Moira fell into step with him as he pushed open the front door.

"Feeling any better?"

The cold air hit his face, making something inside of him snap to attention. Braced, he turned to look at her. What was she doing, walking out of the bar right behind him? Hadn't he just left her in the middle of a gaggle of admirers?

"What do you mean, better?"

Moira decided to forego the banter they usually exchanged. This deserved a serious moment.

"You had this awful look on your face when I came into the video room at the precinct. Like someone had been trying to suck out your soul. I thought that maybe if you hung around your friends, you'd feel better."

Stone sober or slightly less than that, she was a hard woman to get a handle on. Just what was her game? "Do you have this frustrated-mother thing going on?"

His tone was defensive, but she wasn't about to get into a war of words with him.

"Maybe. I've always mothered people, as far back as I can remember." It had begun with her father and sister. She couldn't remember a time when she hadn't played the role. "And the only time I get frustrated is when people try to pretend they don't need a little looking after."

He blew out a breath and found that he had to work at being indignant. "And you think I do."

"Everyone does."

He decided to turn the tables on her, fully expecting to hear her denial. "How about you? Do you need mothering?"

She never looked away. Moira slipped her arm through his, thinking that she'd seen him looking steadier. "Everyone does," she repeated.

Chapter Ten

An empty taxi drove down the darkened street, slowing down, then stopping at the light. Moira noticed Shaw looking toward it as if he were debating hailing the cab. She knew that his own car was in the lot. They'd come here in two cars. She'd driven herself over, following him and Reese.

"Why don't I drive you home?" Even as she made the offer, she wondered if he would take offense. But she knew for a fact that he'd had at least two beers, if not more. He wasn't the reckless kind.

The light had already turned and the cab was driving off, beyond hailing. Shaw slanted a glance at her as he buried his hands deep into his pockets. "Are you saying that you think I can't drive?"

Moira looked up at him, the soul of innocence. "I'm saying that I think you're entertaining that thought. You were the one looking at a cab," she pointed out.

As far as evenings went, it had been an unusual one. None of his siblings or cousins had put in an appearance at the Shannon tonight except for Dax and he had left early, saying something about a date. Shaw had a hunch that the rest of his family were taking turns dropping by the house, giving his dad moral support. A sliver of guilt pricked at him.

Maybe he'd go over tomorrow, he thought, but his afternoon had left a hollow place within him and he knew he wouldn't be much company tonight.

Shaw glanced back at the bar behind him. He supposed he could always have Reese drop him off, but from what he'd witnessed earlier, he had a feeling that his partner was going to be otherwise occupied for a while, possibly for the remainder of the night. Perhaps Reese was finally making some headway with the officer who'd caught his eye last month. Good for Reese.

Not so good for him.

His shoulders moved up and down in a careless shrug. "Better safe than sorry," he agreed, banking down more than a little reluctance. "You appear to be more sober than I feel."

For her part, Moira had indulged in one mixed

drink, a Mai Tai, then spent the evening with her fingers wrapped around a glass of ginger ale. She found that a clear head always served her best when she was trying to absorb information. And that was what this whole evening had been about—absorbing information.

And maybe, just maybe, being around Shaw.

She led the way to her car.

"I didn't think you'd be this sensible." Moira paused, waiting until he buckled up before she turned the key in the ignition.

Belatedly, Shaw reached over to his left. Finding no seat belt there, he frowned. He really was a little muddled, he upbraided himself. How the hell had that happened? He was usually good about policing himself.

Swallowing a curse, he reached over to the right and pulled the seat belt around, buckling up. "Not used to sitting in this seat," he muttered.

"I had a feeling. Don't worry—" she started up the car "—I'll have you home soon."

She didn't drive fast. That surprised him. His eyes shifted slightly in her direction. "You really do like to mother people, don't you?"

Moira shrugged as she just made it through the intersection before the light changed. "Honestly? I never much thought about it. It's just something that comes naturally, I guess." She could tell he wanted more. She decided she liked this slightly inebriated version of him. He was more human. "My father's a wonderful man, but he was more of a friend than a parent to my sister and me. He let details slide.''

''Details?''

Everything but making money, she thought fondly. Where was her father these days? she wondered. More than once she'd regretted taking her stand with him—because it hadn't made her father come around and it had cost her the pleasure of his company. She missed him. A lot.

''Details,'' she repeated. ''Bills he forgot to pay, refrigerator shelves he forgot to fill, laundry he forgot to do. So, if Carrie and I didn't want to be dirty and hungry with bill collectors banging on the door at all hours of the day and night, someone had to take over.''

''And you volunteered.''

She didn't remember ever volunteering. It was something that had just happened. ''Case of natural selection, really. Carrie had no head for figures, no patience. Besides,'' she added philosophically, ''I was older.''

There wasn't much traffic on the streets, and they were almost at his apartment. He liked being with her, he realized.

Boy, he had to be worse off than he thought.

''Eleven months doesn't really count for that much unless you're in the animal kingdom,'' he pointed out.

The comparison made her laugh. Moira stepped

down on the accelerator, beating out another light about to turn red.

She glanced at him, expecting a comment about her driving. But his expression didn't change. "I guess in a way we were. Certainly involved survival of the fittest." She saw him watching her. "Don't get me wrong. I loved my life. Except for missing my mother, I wouldn't have changed a thing."

"Nothing?"

She smiled, sparing him a long glance before looking back at the road. "Well, maybe I would have stayed in Mrs. Brickman's tenth-grade speech class a little longer, but nothing else."

Mrs. Brickman's class. Shaw concentrated hard, staring at her profile. He still had trouble placing her in that scenario.

Maybe it was the beer, but as he stared at her, he found that the curve of her lips, her smile, wove a spell over him.

There was no other word for it. *A spell.*

Magic.

Tonight, for some reason, there was something incredibly intimate about sharing this car ride with her. The world beyond the vehicle was dark, with equally spaced-apart street lamps lighting the way.

It was dark within the car, as well, a velvety darkness that stirred him and made his mind wander down roads Shaw knew he wouldn't be traveling if he'd been stone-cold sober.

He didn't know if the beer had loosened his inhibitions, or just paralyzed what passed for his common sense, tossing it out the window. Or maybe he was just searching for a way to feel clean again after dealing with all the filth he'd had to sift through this afternoon.

All he knew was that he wanted to be with Moira. To have her sitting beside him a while longer and be able to inhale that fragrance that he'd never smelled before, the one that took a swizzle stick to his blood and stirred it all up.

Moira turned into his garden apartment complex. It looked different to her at night. Lonelier. Or maybe she was the one who was lonelier.

She pushed away the thought.

There was a guest space open right before his apartment. She wondered if it was an omen, then decided she was deliberately looking for one. An empty space was an empty space, nothing more. She pulled up into it, smooth as a butter knife cutting through whipped cream.

"Looks like we're here," she announced brightly. "See, I told you this wouldn't take long."

It had taken far too short a time. About to get out, Shaw hesitated, knowing full well that if he were in complete control of his faculties, he would have already been out of the car and halfway up the stairs.

He wasn't sure which was the good thing and which wasn't.

"Do you want to come in?" he asked.

She took his invitation the only way she felt she

could, given the kind of man she'd found Shaw Cavanaugh to be. He wasn't like some of the other officers she'd interacted with these past few days. He didn't regard her as a movie star, or even, she had a hunch, as a woman. More than likely, he still viewed her as the albatross the chief of detectives had tied around his neck. That meant Shaw didn't want to spend one extra minute in her company than he absolutely had to.

Which in turn meant he was asking her to come up to his apartment for only one reason. "Do you need help negotiating the stairs?"

He looked at her for a long moment. "The stairs," he finally said, "are not what I figure I'll have trouble negotiating."

She was out of the car, moving around to his side, wondering if his pride was getting in the way of the truth. She hadn't watched how many drinks he'd had or hadn't had, but the fact that he'd allowed her to drive him home had spoken volumes to her.

Whether he looked it or not, the man had to be three sheets to the wind and ready to be blown away.

"Oh?" As he got out and rose to his feet, Moira subtly presented her shoulder to him just in case he felt the need to lean on something. "Then what will you have trouble negotiating?"

Already his common sense, his sense of self-preservation, was stepping in, preventing him from leaving any side of himself exposed. And airing feelings, airing needs, meant leaving that flank vulnerable. He closed ranks.

"I'm talking too much." Shaw shook his head.

Deftly, she positioned herself so that she was just beneath his arm, slipping it along her shoulders for leverage. That he left it in place told her he really needed help. She lightly grasped his wrist, anchoring him down as best she could.

"Makes up for those bouts of silence you keep subjecting me to," she countered cheerfully. Taking the stairs slowly, she managed to get Shaw up to his apartment door in less time than she thought it would take.

Shaw stared at the door. His door, right? He was closer to feeling no pain than he'd thought. One minute they were in her car, the next, he was standing in front of his door. He'd thought he'd been careful and had not consumed too much tonight. Obviously, he was wrong. The fact that he was letting her help him like this told Shaw that he was worse off then he'd believed.

She felt soft against him, soft and pliant, and he wanted her, he realized as they came to a stop before his door.

Wanted her a great deal.

Knock it off. She's a movie star, a make-believe person.

Shaw dug into his pocket and took out his keys. The proper one never made it into the keyhole. The ring of keys slipped through his fingers, landing before his feet with a soft thud as it came in contact with a flowery welcome mat.

Moira bent down to pick the keys up, noting the design on the mat. She glanced at him as she rose back to her feet. "Not your style. A gift from a girlfriend?"

He laughed. It had been a very long time since he'd had a relationship with a woman that lasted long enough for him to apply the title of "girlfriend" to her.

"Callie, my sister," he corrected. "She thinks I should be friendlier."

"She might be on to something there."

Taking the only key on the ring that looked as if it might fit, she slipped it into the lock. Turning it, Moira congratulated herself on guessing correctly. And then, turning around to hand the keys back to him, Moira suddenly found herself the recipient of a warm, tender kiss that began its transformation the moment contact was made.

It was anything but tender, anything but soft.

Urgency arrived in an ambulance, accompanied by flashing lights and sirens.

She forgot to breathe.

Forgot to do anything but hold on for the ride of her life and hope that she would emerge whole once it was over. Or maybe that didn't even matter, as long as she was there for the ride,

For the life of him, Shaw couldn't begin to explain what came over him. For reasons he couldn't fathom, his self-control had taken a holiday, leaving nothing in its place that remotely resembled it.

Instead, he felt longing. Longing and desire and a myriad of urges he'd had no idea were lurking in the shadows, waiting for a chance to spring out.

He had to kiss her. There was no other choice, no other path.

Shaw didn't remember opening the door, didn't remember crossing the threshold. But somehow, while his lips were sealed to hers, while he was drawing life-affirming sustenance into his veins, he found himself within the apartment.

The door slammed shut behind them.

They were alone. A distant street lamp and the moonlight provided the only illumination within the small living room.

If he'd ever wanted anyone this much before, he couldn't remember when. It was almost as if, by being with her, by giving up control, he borrowed a little protection for himself. It allowed him to deny what he had endured this afternoon.

Her heart doing a fair imitation of a basketball in play during a championship game, Moira pulled her head back. She had the vague sense of trying to collect shattered nerve endings that were scattered from here to God only knew where.

She'd thought that he wanted no part of her. Boy, had she called this shot wrong.

Moira tried for humor, for sanity, succeeding only marginally. "Good thing I was the one who drove you home. If you'd given this kind of a tip to the cabbie, you might have had a lot of explaining to do.''

He framed her face with his hands. He'd noticed from the start that she was beautiful, but beautiful had never had much of an effect on him. So why was it that the very sight of her jarred him clear down to the bone? ''The cabbie wouldn't have made me feel as if I'm in the center of a whirlpool, paddling madly to save myself from certain destruction.''

''And I do?''

His eyes remained on hers. Right now, he wouldn't have been able to explain why he was still standing, not when his knees felt as if they were made of cotton swabs. Wet cotton swabs.

''You do.''

Moira pressed her lips together. It was hard to hear herself think above the wild pounding of her heart. ''I don't know whether I am being complimented or insulted.''

''You don't have to be, either. Just be,'' he whispered, the words, the plea, dancing along her lips a moment before he kissed her again.

He was numbing and inflaming her senses all at the same time. If her life depended on it, she couldn't tell which way was up, which way was down, only that she couldn't breathe and that she didn't care.

The only thing she wanted was for this to go on. For him to make love to her. *With* her.

She wanted to rip the shirt off his body. Instead, Moira wrapped her arms around him, kissing him back for all she was worth. Feeling her body tingling, anticipating, wanting. His body was hard against hers, silently telling her that he wasn't made of stone, that she had affected him as much as he had affected her.

The difference was, she knew, that her effect on him was strictly physical while his on her… Well, it went beyond things that could be seen, that could be touched. Something within her was reacting to him on a level she'd thought she'd shut down a long time ago.

The land of make-believe was perfect for her, because any time she had an excess of emotions, she could spend them there, invest them in a character and work her way through those emotions until they were completely gone again. Until she could go on, unencumbered.

Acting kept her safe, out of harm's way. Because loving someone put her directly in the path of harm. She'd had her heart broken once, by someone who'd just used her. Once was all it took to convince her. Never again.

She wasn't so convinced now.

And she wasn't playing a part now, either. Not yet. She was herself, she was Moira McCormick and she had needs that refused to wait.

Oh, they might have, had this tall, dark, brooding police detective not done this, had he not broken down the door to her private, inner sanctum and pulled her out of hiding.

But he had, and there was no use in speculating about what might have happened if things were different. If he hadn't laid his lips to hers. If he hadn't made the blood rush through her veins.

If he hadn't made her want him.

Eager, her body heating at an incredible rate, she rushed into the pleasure he generated. Rushed to take shelter in his arms, in his ardor, and pretended, just for a little while, that here was someone to take care of her for a change, someone who could take the lead and make her feel protected, safe.

Cared for.

Thousands of fans adored her, loved her, sent tons of letters saying as much, but none of it was real. It was the persona they followed, they adored—not her. Because the real Moira McCormick was not the larger-than-life actress who adorned the movie screens; she wasn't the take-charge woman others looked to for guidance and leadership. The real Moira McCormick was still a frightened child, waiting for her father to come home to her and her sister to wise up.

Her arms tightened around Shaw.

The press of her body against his was causing wild, delicious sensations to race up and down and all through him, breeding more sensations until he couldn't keep track of them, couldn't think. Could only react.

He couldn't get enough of her. The more he kissed her, the more he needed to.

Without thinking things through, without putting roadblocks up for himself that he knew were necessary in order to maintain who and what he was, Shaw allowed himself to live just for the moment.

Because this moment was wondrous.

She made him feel as if he were on fire and she was both his salvation and his doom.

But that was for a thinking man to reason out and he couldn't even remember his social security number or how to tie his shoes. All he remembered, all he knew, was that she was here with him and he wanted her. Wanted to make love with her and feel every inch of her body, hot, throbbing, moist, against his.

Clothing disappeared as the eagerness within him mounted at a prodigious rate. By the way Moira twisted and turned against him, he knew she felt the same way. She returned his urgent kisses with eager ones of her own.

Undergarments went flying, tangling together as the silent race continued. Until they were both dressed only in desire.

She took his breath away.

Her body was firm, taut and pliant, just as he knew it would be. It inflamed him just to touch her, to pass his hands over her tender flesh, curbing the urgency that rushed through him. Seeking to caress, to arouse, to worship. She felt so delicate, he was afraid that he would hurt her.

Moira felt him drawing his hand away. She arched against his palm, holding it in place against her breasts. Loving the way it felt against her skin.

"I won't break," she murmured against his mouth.

"But I might," he whispered back. She made him ache so much, he was surprised that he hadn't shattered into a million pieces already. He would work through the insanity of this situation later. All he knew now was that if he had to stop, if he couldn't have her, he would explode.

Pulling her onto the floor, he continued kissing her, continued familiarizing himself with every inch of her. And as he did so, he knew he was drawing a life force from her that infused him with a sense of power and humility that made his head spin.

Lacing his fingers through hers, Shaw shifted his body until he was over her, kissing her over and over again. He felt her opening for him, felt her arching her hips in a silent, heated invitation.

Shaw plunged himself into her, initiating a rhythm she echoed. He felt her gasp against him as the tempo increased, felt as if a blazing chariot raced after him as he hurried to find the summit he sought.

Her nails dug into the back of his hands, urging him on. She made noises against his mouth.

Whether they were words, his name, he didn't know. They tasted of sweetness and sex.

And triumph as the moment carried them both away, then let them find their own ground.

Chapter Eleven

Euphoria slowly melted back into the shadows, leaving the stark shades of reality in its wake. Moira felt a chill slipping around her shoulders.

Turning her head, she looked at Shaw. He was beside her on the floor, his arm tucked around her. His profile gave no indication of the thoughts that were going on inside his head.

What *was* he thinking? That he'd just made it with a movie star? That she had sex indiscriminately with any man who was available whenever the whim hit? More than anything, she didn't want him believing that. As far as sex went, she was almost a novice.

"I just want you to know, I don't do this normally." Her voice was small.

His mouth curved slightly as he slanted a glance at her face. "Seemed normal to me."

She raised herself up on her elbow, not sure whether he was teasing her. "No. I mean I don't sleep around. Despite what you might think about people in my profession, this isn't the way I usually behave."

Shaw laughed softly to himself. "Then I guess I got lucky."

"Shaw—"

He cut her off. This wasn't a time for apologies or explanations. "Moira."

Flustered, not sure whether she was saying too much or not enough, Moira bit the word off and spat it out. "What?"

"Shut up." Before she could protest, he'd brought her face down to his and kissed her. When she drew back, confused, he said, "You don't have to explain anything. This doesn't need subtitles."

This had meant something to her. She didn't want him thinking that she expected anything, but she wanted him to know that. That this night had been different. "I just want you to know—"

She looked as if she were in agony, searching for the right words. Some things were best left unsaid. He laid a finger to her lips, stopping the flow.

"I know."

Moira looked at him uncertainly. "You do?"

Shaw cupped her cheek. A strange fondness poured through his veins. "Hey, I'm a police detective. That means I do have some working instincts. Intuition, if you will."

Something inside her felt like laughing and crying at the same time. "I thought that was a female thing."

He ran his hand along her body, his eyes smiling softly into hers. She couldn't begin to guess at what he was thinking and told herself that maybe it was better that way. Better to enjoy rather than to have everything orchestrated ahead of time.

"Definitely a female thing," he murmured, his mind definitely not on a thought process.

Lowering her back onto the floor, Shaw drew her to him, his body hungry again. He knew this was a single night and that tomorrow things would be different. But he didn't want to let tonight go, didn't want to move on just yet. Not when he wanted her again, wanted the sensation she created within him again. She made him feel as if he were going over the falls in a barrel. No other woman had ever done that for him and he wanted to savor the wild ride one more time.

But as he felt his body heating, the sound of ringing penetrated the mist about his brain. Duty above pleasure. Reluctantly, he drew his head back, listening. It *was* ringing.

"Damn it." From his vantage point above her, Shaw looked around, trying to locate his jacket. He was vaguely aware of leaving his cell phone in one of the pockets.

With equal reluctance, Moira rejoined the world. A moment later, she identified the sound. ''No, that's my 'Damn it,' not yours.'' He looked at her curiously. ''My cell phone rings like Morse code,'' she explained.

Placing her hands against his chest, Moira pushed lightly. He obliged by moving out of her way. Sitting up, she zeroed in on the sound as the phone rang again.

Her phone was in her purse, which was buried under the heap comprised of his clothes and hers. Digging, Moira located the bag and drew it over to her, aware that he was watching her every move.

Aware that his gaze made her hotter by the moment.

It took effort to collect her thoughts and concentrate on the cell phone in her hand. ''Hello?''

''Moira, I'm sorry.''

She stiffened, recognizing her sister's voice. Recognizing the abject misery in it. Something was very, very wrong. Had she gone back to Simon? She saw Shaw looking at her, the detective in him coming alive.

''Sorry?'' Moira tried to sound as upbeat as possible. ''Sorry about what, Carrie? What's the matter?''

She heard her sister crying on the other end before

Carrie finally hiccuped and said, "I messed up, I messed up bad."

Moira's mind scrambled over a dozen different scenarios, swiftly examining and discarding all of them. There was no point in speculating. Whatever she feared had to be put side. Carrie needed her strength. "Listen to me, Carrie. There's nothing that you've done that can't be undone or fixed."

She heard Carrie sob on the other end. "No, no, you can't fix this, Moira. Only I can. And I will. I won't be a problem to you anymore."

Fear gripped her heart. This sounded bad, very bad. In this frame of mind, Carrie could do something drastic. Moira knew that. "Where are you, baby? Talk to me, Carrie. Where are you?" She struggled to keep her own hysteria out of her voice.

She heard Carrie gulp. "I'm at the hotel, but I won't be a problem much longer, Moira. I promise."

Oh, God, was she going to do something to herself? Moira gripped the cell with both hands, as if that could somehow keep Carrie from doing herself harm.

"You're not a problem, you're my sister. I love you." She searched for the right combination of words that would bring her sister around. "Whatever it is, we'll handle it together." Quickly, she began getting dressed, holding the cell against her shoulder with her ear. "Just stay there. I'll be right over. Promise me you won't do anything until I get there. Do you hear me? Carrie? Carrie?''

The line went dead.

Dazed, scared, Moira looked up and saw that Shaw was already dressed, without a hint of softness in his eyes. He handed over her skirt and shoes. ''Let's go,'' he told her.

''You don't have to—''

''From the sound of it, you could do with a detective clearing your path for you.'' Shaw strapped his service revolver on.

From nowhere, tears materialized in her eyes, fighting to spill out. ''Thank you.''

Grabbing his keys, he eased her out and closed the door behind him. ''Don't,'' he warned. ''It's just part of my job.''

But she knew it wasn't.

Moira's heart was in her throat the entire short-lived trip to the hotel. True to his word, Shaw got them there in an incredibly short amount of time. Her heart still felt like a boulder lodged in a tight space.

She had no idea what to expect when she burst into her hotel suite. All the calls she'd placed to the room from the time Carrie had hung up on her until they'd reached the hotel had gone unanswered. Had Carrie left? And how had she left—using the door or by other means?

Moira was afraid to let her mind stray too far from

the moment, from the thought that she had to reach Carrie before something terrible happened.

She refused to allow herself to believe that it already had.

"Carrie, Carrie, where are you?" she called to her sister the second she was in the suite. Trying to sound calm, Moira felt utterly frantic inside.

There was no answer.

And then Shaw tapped on her shoulder, pointing to the billowing curtains.

The window was open.

Fear squeezed her heart as she raced to the window. She couldn't remember her mouth ever feeling this dry.

"Carrie?"

Looking out the window, she saw that her sister was standing on the ledge a little more than ten feet away from her. Carrie's body trembled as she stared straight ahead. When she looked toward the window, she wavered slightly. Moira swallowed a gasp, afraid to make any sudden noises.

"Go away, Moira," Carrie pleaded. "I've got to make things right."

Sheer terror seized Moira. She was only vaguely aware of Shaw being behind her in the room. She couldn't believe that this was happening. Not with Carrie at the center of this drama. Carrie had always been so happy-go-lucky, so full of life. What had that bastard done to break her sister's spirit this way?

"By jumping?" Moira demanded.

"It's the only way."

Moira leaned out the window, not knowing what her next move was, only that she had to save Carrie somehow. And then she felt two strong hands on either side of her waist, moving her back into the room as if she weighed nothing. She glared at Shaw. "What are you doing?" she demanded.

Shaw didn't waste time answering her. Instead, he took her place at the window. And then the next moment, he was climbing out onto the ledge.

"Are you crazy?" Moira cried.

Carrie turned her head to see what was happening. Her eyes widened when she saw the man who had come to her sister's rescue the other night.

"Go away. Please go away," Carrie begged.

"You don't want to jump, Carrie." Shaw's voice was low, soothing. Authoritative.

Tears slid down Carrie's cheeks. She turned her face forward. "Yes, I do. This is the only way I can fix everything."

"You're not fixing anything," he told her. "You jump, your pain will be over, but Moira's will haunt her until the moment she takes her last breath."

"I'm doing this for Moira," Carrie sobbed. "This isn't her fault. It's mine and I have to make it right."

Ever so slightly, so that he didn't call attention to the fact, Shaw moved a little closer to the woman. "You know better than that. Moira won't see it that way. You jump, she'll think she failed you somehow.''

''No, me,'' Carrie cried. ''I failed me. I failed her.'' Her voice broke.

Moira thought her heart would break. How could everything suddenly be falling apart like this? An hour ago, she'd been happier than she ever remembered being, now everything threatened to turn into ashes around her.

''Why are you doing this, Carrie?'' she cried, leaning out the window.

Carrie tried to see her and almost lost her footing. With a scream, she pressed herself against the building. ''Because I'm pregnant, Moira. I'm pregnant.''

That bastard, Moira thought. ''Does Simon know?''

Carrie sobbed. ''Simon doesn't want the baby, doesn't want me. He said he only wanted me because he thought that it was a way to get to you, to your money. When I told him there was no way, he left.'' Despair echoed in every syllable she uttered. ''I'm sorry, Moira. I'm so sorry.''

''Sorry that you've got lousy taste in men?'' Moira made it sound completely inconsequential. ''We'll work on it. But I've always wanted to be an aunt. Please, Carrie, please come in. I'll take care of you, I'll take care of the baby. Please don't do this.''

Carrie took a deep breath, as if she were wrestling with herself. And then, finally, she murmured, ''All right.''

But then nothing happened.

Her sister looked like a deer frozen in the glare of the headlights of an oncoming car. "Carrie?"

"I can't move, Moira," Carrie cried. "I can't move."

"Don't look down, Carrie," Shaw ordered. "Look straight ahead." There was about four feet between them. "I'm coming to get you."

"No, no," Carrie cried, panicking. "Stay where you are. We'll both fall."

"Not today. Not if you listen to me." His heels against the wall, Shaw moved slowly toward her until he was within arm's length of her. As Moira held her breath, Shaw stretched his hand out toward the younger woman. "See, here's my hand. Can you feel my fingers?"

Plastered against the wall, eyes fixed on the top of the tall building in the distance, Carrie seemed afraid to breathe. "Yes."

"Okay, this is going to be slow." He spoke to her as if he were trying to gentle a wild deer, knowing that any sudden move on her part could be the last for both of them. "I'm going to work my fingers along your hand until I've got your wrist. Then you're going to move your feet—very slowly—sideways."

"I can't," Carrie sobbed.

"Yes, you can," Moira told her firmly. "You can do this, Carrie."

"We've got all night," Shaw said quietly, "so you don't have to hurry."

"Yes, I do." Carrie's voice quavered. "I have to go to the bathroom."

It was so ludicrous, so fundamental, he almost laughed. "Then maybe you'll move a little faster. The pace is yours, Carrie."

She ventured a look down. Gasping, she tried to melt even farther against the wall. "I'll fall."

"I won't let you fall, Carrie."

There were tears in Carrie's voice. They matched the ones clawing in Moira's throat. "You promise?"

"I promise," Shaw insisted.

Moira held her breath, watching. Praying. It felt as if everything was happening in slow motion.

Holding Carrie's wrist, talking her through every second, Shaw worked his way back along the ledge inch by torturous inch.

They were almost there when her sister took a misstep, her foot slipping. For a horrendous moment, it looked as if it was all over, as if Carrie would plunge from the ledge, taking Shaw with her.

Moira's heart stopped. She'd never felt so helpless in her life.

And then, miraculously, it was over. Shaw had edged his way back into the hotel suite, his fingers locked in an iron grip around Carrie's wrist. Less than a second later, Carrie was inside the room, as well.

The moment she came through the window, Carrie sank to her knees, every bone in her body liquefying. She began to sob.

Moira was there to throw her arms around her sister, holding the younger woman to her.

"It's all right, Carrie, it's all right. The worst is over." Moira looked over her sister's head at Shaw. She knew enough about the law to know that all attempted suicides were supposed to be reported. She didn't want Carrie being taken into custody, not when her emotions were so fragile. "Right?"

He understood her meaning perfectly. "Right. Why don't you help your sister into the bathroom?"

Nodding, she helped Carrie up to her feet, then took her to the bathroom. Leaving her there, Moira came out and closed the door behind her.

She searched Shaw's face. "You don't have to report this, do you?"

"I should, but..." He shook his head. "She's got enough to deal with. Just make sure she doesn't try this kind of thing again, because then I will report it. For her own good."

"I understand." She allowed herself a smile as she looked at him. When she thought of what could have happened tonight, her blood ran cold. But everything had turned out all right. Because he had insisted on coming with her. "You realize you're my hero, don't you?"

"Why?" A hint of a smile played on his lips. "Because I went out on a ledge for you?" In more ways than one, he added silently, thinking of earlier.

She'd made him emotionally vulnerable and he wasn't sure how he felt about that.

"Yeah."

Taking hold of his lapels, she rose on her toes and kissed him with all the pent-up emotions churning inside of her, seeking release. The kiss threatened to ignite right there.

He let it go on as long as he dared. Backing up, Shaw blew out a breath.

"One more like that and I'm not going to be able to leave." And then he looked over her shoulder toward the bathroom. There were more important things going on tonight than satisfying his reawakened sex drive. "You going to be all right with her?"

Pressing her lips together, she nodded. "I think the worst is over. When you got her to agree to come back in, I knew we'd be all right."

He told himself to get going. He found himself lingering instead, taking her hands in both of his. Lengthening the moment and hardly recognizing himself. "Did you mean what you said about always wanting to be an aunt?"

The smile began in her eyes, or maybe her inner core, ultimately shining on her face. "I love kids."

"Putting that mothering instinct of yours to work," he guessed. He didn't want to explore the other feeling that had just popped up, the one of wanting to share children with her. He'd never wanted kids before. Where the hell had that come from?

"Something like that." He released her hands. She walked him to the door, wishing he could remain. Knowing he couldn't. Carrie needed her. Whatever else was going on right now was going to have to wait. "Here, take my car." She handed him the keys.

"Don't you need it?"

She shook her head. "I'll have someone drive me." She looked at him, tears coming into her eyes. "I don't know how to thank you."

He took the keys she offered. Standing on the threshold, he ran his thumb along her lower lip. And felt something quickening inside of him. "You already did."

"I'll see you tomorrow morning." He looked at her blankly. "The ride-along," she prompted. "It's my last day." A pang accompanied the words.

"Yeah, right," he muttered, turning away. Somehow that fact had gotten lost tonight. "Call me if she uses the window to go out and get a breath of fresh air," he told her as he walked down the hall. If he turned around to look at her, he knew he wouldn't leave.

"I'll do that," Moira promised. She heard the bathroom door opening behind her. "But I don't think it'll be necessary."

How had a week gone by that fast, he wondered as he walked down the hall to the elevator. He reminded himself that he'd been the one who'd wanted it to sail by in the first place.

Be careful what you wish for.

Truer words had never been written, he decided as he got into the elevator.

Shaw watched her walking toward him, absorbing every nuance, every sway of her hips. He'd come to the precinct early, just to be in this chair, taking in this view. "So how is she?"

Moira was touched that he cared enough to ask. "I left her with Edwin. He's in charge of preproduction," she was quick to explain. "Edwin will keep Carrie busy all day." She'd told him to do as much.

He raised a skeptical eyebrow. "Lot of work being a stand-in?"

Moira smiled. Because Reese wasn't there yet, she sat down in the chair next to Shaw's desk.

"There will be for her. Carrie and I were up half the night, making plans for the new baby. By tonight, she's going to be so exhausted, the only place she'll feel like crawling to is bed." Reaching over the desk, she put her hand on his. "I really can't thank you enough for last night."

Coming to join them, Reese stopped dead. He looked from one to the other, clearly feeling out of the loop and convinced he knew which way that loop was swaying. "I miss something last night?"

Moira never missed a beat. "I was talking about

going to the Shannon. It had such wonderful atmosphere. Perfect for the movie.''

''It was my idea to take you there,'' Reese reminded her.

''Yes, it was, and I really should be thanking you, not him.''

Reese slowly nodded his head, not completely taken in. ''Maybe. Unless there's something else to be thanking him for.''

This time, Shaw was the one who stepped up. ''The pleasure of my company.''

''Ha. That'll be the day.'' Reese hooted. ''You know—'' his voice dropped to a confidential level ''—I don't know about my partner, but I'm going to miss having you ride along with us.''

''Thank you.'' She rose, ready to get started. ''By the way, we are doing some local shooting and if it's all right with your captain, we could use you and Shaw and some of the others as extras.''

Reese grinned from ear to ear, tickled by the idea. ''Sounds good to me.''

She noticed that Shaw made no comment. Just as he hadn't attempted to add anything about missing her once she was gone. She was surprised that it bothered her, but told herself that it was just his way, that he'd more than proven himself by what he'd done for her sister. As for the other, well, she knew there were no strings attached to their relationship.

As she walked out with the two men for the last time, Moira found herself longing for strings.

Chapter Twelve

Shaw waited until the bartender refilled Moira's glass and then moved on to serve someone else before he made his observation.

"You look disappointed."

They'd been here for close to an hour, most of the time being spent with her telling the officers who dropped by the table that she truly felt privileged to have taken part in their world for the past week. Stopping at the Shannon had come at the end of rather an uneventful day. They had followed leads that had gone nowhere. Shaw and his partner were no further along in their investigation than they had been several days ago.

Yes, she thought, she was disappointed. For more reasons than one. But she hadn't thought it showed that obviously. She offered him a self-depreciating smile. "I was hoping for some spectacular bust to cap off my week's career."

Shaw pushed aside his beer. The half-full glass was his second of the evening and his limit. He got more of a kick just looking at her.

He shared her disappointment, but he knew the case would come together by and by. He wasn't about to back off until it did. "You spend months, years on some cases, gathering information, putting things in place, and then, when you least expect it and aren't looking, things align themselves just right."

She felt a shiver sliding down her back. For a moment, the rest of the people in the small, friendly bar seemed to fade into the walls. "Are you talking about a bust, or love?"

He laughed softly, looking into his glass and watching the lights dance around on the pale amber liquid. "A bust. Why?"

She gave a half shrug. It had to be her state of mind. She was reading too much into things. "Because the same words could be applied to love. If I believed in love," she added.

Shaw studied her for a long moment. The question, he knew, was loaded. But he couldn't make himself walk away from it. "You don't believe in love?"

Her smile found him where he lived, then undulated up and down through his system.

"I sell make-believe for a living." She thought of her unorthodox childhood. "I always have, as far back as I can remember." And because she did, there were times when she felt as if nothing was real. Like now. "Love is a sleight of hand, an illusion."

"Damn, but that sounds awfully dark for someone so sunny." He leaned over the table, creating an aura of intimacy within a crowd of people. "Or is that sunniness an illusion, too?"

There was a sadness in her this evening that caused her to be more introspective than normal. She realized that she really didn't want this to end. That she wanted to go on seeing Shaw.

Her own weakness upset her.

"Partially," she admitted. "For my own sake. If I keep on smiling, keep on projecting positive thoughts, maybe I'll buy into it, too." Her mouth curved. "At least for a little while."

Moira paused to sip a little more of the ginger ale she'd ordered. Someone came up to the table and asked her to sign an autograph. She obliged, signing one of the napkins as she took the time to talk to the burly man, saying how much she admired *his* work.

"Keeping the peace, keeping people safe, doesn't stop because someone yells 'Cut,' at the end of the day." She handed the man the napkin. "You're on duty 24/7. I don't know how you do it."

The policeman went away grinning from ear to ear, holding the napkin as if it had turned into something precious.

Shaw leaned back, watching the man rejoin his friends. "Well, he's a lifelong fan now." He turned back around to face her. "I don't think his feet were touching the floor when he walked away."

She made no comment about the patrolman's reaction. "I meant what I said. I don't know how you do it. How you manage to fit in a life with all you do."

Shaw had been around it all his life. It had been the one bone of contention between his parents. His mother always felt his father spent too much time with his cases, not enough time with his family. His father had only managed to change his ways after his mother had disappeared.

"You have to want to," he told her simply.

And the funny thing was, he was finding himself wanting to. Maybe it was because she wasn't pushing for anything that he found himself thinking along those lines, he honestly didn't know. All he knew was that when she finally left, he was going to miss her a great deal more than he ever thought he would.

But "finally" wasn't here yet and he was going to concentrate on the moment.

Shaw moved closer to her, so that he didn't have

to shout. His question was only for her. "So, now what happens?"

She thought of her schedule. "We start shooting Monday."

"No. I mean *now.*" He looked at her, emphasizing the word.

Anticipation whispered through her. She ran her thumb along the glass's moist side, leaving a trail. "I'm going to finish my ginger ale and go to my hotel room." Moira raised her eyes to his. "Unless I get a better suggestion."

He wanted to take her home, but even that wasn't simple. There were other things to consider. "What about your sister?"

That he gave any thought to Carrie's situation touched her more than she could ever begin to put into words. "Edwin took up most of her day and now I have her busy rehabilitating Amy."

According to the preproduction assistant, when she called him earlier today, the two girls, both needy in different ways, had hit it off immediately on the set. Moira had been quick to act on it, calling Carrie and asking for her "help" in keeping Amy from thinking about returning to the street. Carrie had been more than interested in hearing Amy's story.

Moira smiled fondly. It had been the perfect solution. "Carrie does very well with projects. I figured this would help them both out."

There was no doubt about it—Moira McCormick

was not just another beautiful face. "You might be right."

Finishing her drink, she placed the glass on the table, pushing it with her fingertip until it butted up against his almost empty one. The next move was his. She knew where she wanted to spend the next part of the evening, but she wasn't about to say it.

He took his cue. Shaw laced his hand through hers. "Let's go."

She looked at him innocently, so innocently that for a moment, he felt as if he'd misread her signals. "Where?"

"My place."

She said nothing, only rose from her chair, her hand remaining in his. He led her out.

Moira was vaguely aware of people moving out of their way as they made their way to the establishment's front door. She was far more aware of her heart rate increasing with each step she took.

They barely made it to his apartment door.

Leaving the Shannon, Moira followed him in her vehicle, feeling that would be the simplest way to go even though she would have rather driven over in the same car, would have rather spent every moment she could in his company. There were precious and few enough of them for her to want to husband every second she could.

The moment she parked her car, she was hurrying

up to the cluster of apartments where his was nestled.

Shaw waited for her at the top of the stairs, his door already open.

Dashing up the flight, when she reached the last step, Moira couldn't help thinking the scene was right out of a movie.

The scent of his cologne filling her head, the sound of crickets chirping in concert somewhere close by in the dark, she flung herself into Shaw's arms, lost herself in his kiss. She allowed the heat that hovered about her to overtake her.

She was vaguely aware that they made it inside, the closing door registering somewhere on the outer perimeter of her brain. The rest of her brain was completely taken up by thoughts of him, by sensations and emotions all associated with him.

Waiting a second longer threatened her sanity. Fingers moving quickly, Moira tore off his clothing. Shirt, pants, shoes—they all went flying, ripped in some places when they offered resistance.

He was gentler with her clothing, undoing buttons, taking time with zippers. Whether it was because she would need them again later to leave his apartment, or because he wasn't on fire in the same way she was, Moira didn't know, and there wasn't enough brain power available to her at the moment for her to sort it out.

All she knew was that since last night, the only

thing she could think about was making love with him again. And again.

But this time, at least part of it was going to be on her terms, she promised herself. She wanted to leave as much of an impression on him as he had left on her. She didn't want to blend in with all the other women who had been in his life.

Who would be in his life after she was gone.

The thought drenched her with an incredible wave of sorrow and she struggled to get past it, all the while doing things to his body that he had done to hers until every secret was unlocked, every inch had been committed to memory through her sense of touch.

The urgency between them grew, embracing them and taking command.

Getting carried away, she wrapped herself around him and pushed him to the floor. She'd managed to jar an end table. There was the sound of something crashing as it found the same level they did.

She didn't bother looking in the direction of the crash. "I'll pay for that," she promised.

She felt his mouth form a smile beneath her lips. "Yeah, you will."

She had a feeling he wasn't talking about money.

Shaw grasped her hips as she moved over him. This was unique. He'd never had a woman take the initiative before, never had a woman take the upper hand. He had no idea what had lit the fire within her, only that its heat was inflaming him, as well. If he had wanted her the first time, his desire had increased tenfold now that he knew what awaited him.

It felt as if everything was happening at fast-forward speed, yet somehow in slow motion, as well. He was aware of every movement, every twist, every repercussion as it echoed through him, making him want more. Making him want *her* more.

He knew it was fantasy, all fantasy. The Cop and the Movie Star. It had make-believe stamped all over it. But just for now, he would allow himself to pretend that the supple woman in his arms was just an ordinary woman, his for the having.

No, that wasn't right, because even if Moira hadn't been who she was, even if the status of celebrity had never touched her life, there was nothing ordinary about Moira. She was extraordinary. Every man's dream.

Certainly his.

And that both excited and scared him. Because eventually, people had to wake up. That was when dreams faded, eventually becoming nothing more than a distant memory.

But all that was tomorrow and everyone knew, tomorrow never came. It was always today, always now.

And for now, he had her the way he wanted her, the way he needed her.

Sweat dripping into his eyes, his body yearning for her, Shaw switched positions until he was over her again, the feel of her perspiration exciting him beyond measure. His eyes on hers, he drove himself into her, seeking shelter, seeking redemption he hadn't known he craved.

The rhythm and the perspiration sealed them to one another, making the journey slick until they crossed into the land they sought.

It felt like hours later that he finally regained the use of his mind. When he did, the awe refused to abate. Her stamina, her need, had shaken him down to his very shoes. He could hardly draw air into his lungs.

He heard her murmur against his ear. "Wow, what *was* that?"

She'd certainly rocked the foundations of his known world. "I don't know, but if we could patent it, we'd make a fortune."

She didn't want to talk; she wanted to curl into the moment and have it last forever. How did she do that without seeming as if she were needy? Without giving him the upper hand? Because he clearly had it.

She resorted to flippancy. It was her only defense. "And let the rest of the world in on it? I don't think so."

She felt him comb his fingers through her hair, moving it away from her face. Did he realize how much that made her tingle? How much it made her ache for him?

"Stay the night?" His breath, his words, slid seductively along her skin.

Of all the things she'd expected him to say, that had never even remotely numbered among them. Elation and fear skipped through her.

Moira raised her head and looked at him, certain that she had misheard. A macho cop like Shaw didn't say things like that. Only men who wrote poetry at least at one time in their lives voiced sentiments like that. "What did you say?"

He'd crossed a line and he knew it. But there was no turning back, at least, not to any visible landmarks. "Stay the night."

She wanted to. Oh, how she wanted to. But that would be indulging herself and she had more than just herself to think about right now.

"I can't. I don't want to leave Carrie alone all night."

They were the words, the sentiments, that could have easily come from any one of his family members. At one point or another, each of them had felt protective of another member. God knew they'd all felt protective of Rayne. And of their father.

He wondered if she realized how much like his own family she was.

"I understand," he murmured, then surprised her by suddenly shifting positions until he was looming over her, his strong arms bracketing her on either side. "I guess that means I'll have to do now what I had planned for later."

Amusement entered her eyes, chasing away the serious moment. "Oh, and what was that?"

His body, hard, ready, slid over hers. But even as it did, he lowered his lips to her throat, gently gliding along her sensitive flesh. Marking her. Making her ready. ''Guess.''

She didn't have to.

He showed her.

When Shaw finally got up out of bed the next morning, an incredible loneliness hung over him, one he'd never experienced before. One he couldn't begin to explain.

It had begun to hover over him the moment Moira left his apartment. Pacing the floor, feeling restless, he'd been unable to find refuge in anything. Flipping on the late-night programs hadn't helped. Nothing distracted him long enough for him to wrap his mind around it.

He'd found himself missing her the moment the sound of her footsteps faded into the night. Even before her car was out of sight.

Well, it was something he was going to have to get used to, he told himself sternly. She was going to be completely gone from his life soon enough. The filming wasn't going to last forever, and once the film company pulled up stakes and returned to their Los Angeles studio, she'd be gone.

And his life would be back to normal.

Whatever the hell that was.

Shaw greeted daylight from the other side, having only dozed a few minutes here and there. Just enough to make him feel as if he'd been pulled inside out and dragged across a bed of cacti in slow motion.

The restlessness grew. Coming out of the shower, he knew if he remained by himself, it was only going to get worse. He needed to be around people. People he'd have to put on a show for unless he wanted them to jump in and start picking apart his problem.

He didn't want it being touched. His problem was something he would handle in time. But that time wasn't now.

Shaw made up his mind. He was going to go stop by his father's place and get lost in the crowd.

Less than an hour later he found himself driving his vehicle down the familiar road to the house where he'd grown up. It was Saturday, so that meant that the full complement was probably set to arrive. Once upon a time, a full complement meant the six of them, his father and his siblings. But now, that number had grown and there was no telling how many people would show up at the table. The more the merrier, he supposed. With enough noise going on, he wouldn't be able to think. Which was exactly what he wanted.

He wanted to stop thinking until he could compartmentalize his thoughts again, the way he had been able to before Moira had come into his life.

She hadn't come into his life, he corrected himself. Their paths had just crossed, that was all.

The hell it was.

Blocking his internal argument, Shaw got out of his car and went up the walk. He braced himself a second before he took out his key to the front door. Until just a minute ago, he'd forgotten that he'd be seeing his mother at the table, as well.

Some son he was, Shaw upbraided himself, forgetting about his mother making a reappearance in their lives after all this time. This thing with Moira really did have him tied up in knots, didn't it?

"You going to pose in front of that door all morning, or are you planning on putting the key into the lock sometime soon?"

He glanced over his shoulder to see Callie standing behind him. He looked around, but saw no one else walking behind her. He rarely saw her here alone. "Where's your better half? Is he starting to get cold feet?"

With the patient smile of a sister accustomed to endless teasing, she said, "That'll be the day. He keeps suggesting we elope instead of having that big family wedding in August. No, Brent had to go in to his office today to get some papers. And Rachel's at a sleepover. I thought I'd come by and give Dad some moral support. By the look on your face, you look as if you could use a little, too."

He stiffened slightly. Sister or not, he didn't like being analyzed. He saw it as an invasion of privacy.

And until he untangled this satisfactorily for himself, what he was wrestling with was most definitely private. "Then you better get your eyes checked. I'm fine."

"Well, nothing's changed about your disposition, I see. Waspish as ever. How's that ride-along going for you?"

Was it his imagination, or did his sister sound a tad too innocent as she asked the question? He unlocked the front door and walked in.

"It's over," he told her, leading the way to the kitchen. "Moira McCormick had her last day in the car yesterday." He looked over his shoulder at his sister, deliberately showing her how unaffected he was by the events. "She goes back to being a movie star on Monday."

Looking into the kitchen, Callie grinned. "I guess that leaves her the weekend to go slumming."

He had no idea what his sister meant by that, but the sooner he got away from the topic of Moira McCormick's actions, the better.

"I guess," he echoed.

Callie tapped him on the shoulder and then pointed into the kitchen.

Following the direction of her finger, he saw that among the people seated around the enormous table in his father's kitchen were two new faces.

Moira and her sister Carrie.

Chapter Thirteen

Andrew turned from the stove in time to see the expression on his oldest son's face as Shaw walked into the kitchen. Stunned was the best description he could apply to it.

"I thought while Moira was in town, she might appreciate a home-cooked meal," he explained mildly.

For once, he wasn't playing matchmaker. This was about Rose and his desperately trying anything to jar her memory, to make her come around. He knew the path back wasn't a straight one and he wasn't above using any ammunition that came his way. When the conversation had gotten around to

Moira McCormick being Shaw's ride-along and Rose had expressed a fondness for the actress's movies, inviting the young woman to his table while she was in Aurora had seemed only natural to Andrew.

"She asked me if she could bring her sister along," Andrew went on, shifting pancakes from the griddle to a large plate. "What could I say? We all know that there's always room for one more."

His father's familiar mantra echoed in his head as Shaw stared at Moira. The latter smiled back at him, her expression the very essence of innocence.

He knew his father needed no excuse to throw open his doors to anyone with half an appetite. He also knew his father had his heart set on marrying all of them off. Now that his brother and sisters were set, Shaw knew that, as the last man standing, he'd become a moving target. But even his father had to know that there was absolutely no future here.

He took his seat, which this morning seemed to be beside Moira instead of Teri the way it usually was. "How did you manage to get through to her?"

Andrew laughed. "Brian gave me the number." He looked at the woman he'd placed at the foot of the table, where she'd always sat before. "Seems that your mother is quite a fan of Moira's movies."

"I've seen every one," Claire told Shaw quietly. "You always portray such strong, independent women."

"But with a soft center," Rayne interjected.

When the others looked at her in surprise, given that she had always pretended to be so disinterested in mundane things like movies, she protested, "Okay, so I've seen a few of them, too."

No one wanted Rayne to feel as if she were squirming on a hook. "It's not like it's some kind of secret vice, Rayne," Teri told her.

"Oh, God, I hope not." Moira laughed. "Otherwise, my career's going to be over soon." When Shaw looked at her quizzically, she explained, "The 'Last Year's Blonde' syndrome. You know, one nondescript face taking the place of another. It's been going on ever since the first movie reel flickered inside of a darkened movie theater." It was a given that in most cases, the staying power of actresses had never been as strong as that of actors. She intended to be the exception.

"I don't think you have to worry about that," Andrew said warmly as he placed a plate filled with French toast drizzled with powdered sugar in front of her. "The last thing you are is nondescript."

To Shaw's surprise, not only did he see Moira smile with pleasure at the compliment, but he thought he actually detected a blush creeping up her neck to her cheeks. It didn't seem possible. Someone like Moira had to be accustomed to receiving compliments by the truckload. At this point, she should have been more than a little jaded about the whole thing. Yet there was that trace of pink along her skin.

Watching her interact with his family, she seemed like just any other woman. Any other woman with a drop-dead face and body, and an eight-figure income.

What the hell was he thinking, telling himself she fit in here? Of course she fit in, she was an actress, she could have seemed to fit in at an eighteenth-century penal colony if the part called for it. This was all an illusion and he had to remind himself of that before he got so entangled that he didn't know which end was up.

If that hadn't happened already.

Finishing a story she'd been telling at Claire's request, about the last movie she'd filmed, a light romantic comedy set in Hawaii, Moira looked at Shaw. As everyone laughed at her punch line, she leaned in to him and whispered, "You're thinking too hard."

"What?"

She feathered her fingertips just above the point where his eyebrows had drawn together. For a precious moment, the other people in the room faded into the background.

"There's a furrow there. I can almost feel the thoughts jumping from one place to another. Relax," she advised softly.

Was he afraid she was going to say or do something to embarrass him? Or was there another reason he looked so intense?

He drew his head back, though not as quickly as he thought he should have. ''I'm not tense.''

She grinned. ''Sure you're not.''

''Something you'd like to share with the class?'' Callie suggested, amused as she looked from Moira to her brother.

Shaw blew out a breath. Sometimes, there was such a thing as too much family. This was one of those moments. ''Not a thing.''

Callie leaned across the table toward Moira. ''He always was the selfish kind, even as a kid.'' Clearly delighted for Shaw, there was no way she could keep a straight face. ''But he does have his good points—if you look hard enough.''

There was no point in playing coy. She liked these people too much and even though she knew she was only living in the moment, Moira wanted them all to know that the moment was a wonderful one.

''I know.''

''Well, don't get carried away,'' Clay advised. ''They're not all *that* good.'' He got a poke in the ribs from his fiancée, Ilene, for his comment. ''No fair,'' he protested, making a face that made his son, Alex, giggle. ''You can't beat me up until after we're married.''

''No, go ahead, Ilene. Beat up on him,'' Teri urged. ''I'll even hold him down for you.''

''You and what army?'' Clay challenged.

''Me,'' Callie volunteered.

"Me, too," Rayne was quick to chime in.

Moira slid a glance toward her sister to see if she was enjoying herself. To her relief, Carrie was laughing at something Teri had just whispered in her ear. Pleased, hopeful, her eyes met Andrew's as he brought another platter of food to the table.

They understood each other, she and Andrew, Moira thought. Their main concern was the people they loved. She knew the entire story about his wife and how he'd gone on looking for her while raising five children, never giving up hope even when everyone else told him to close that chapter and get on with his life. She could only guess at what he was going through now. The old saying, "So near and yet so far," occurred to her.

Moira wished that her father could have known Andrew. Maybe, under Andrew's influence, Matthew McCormick could have become the father she knew in her heart he was.

But there was no point in wishing for a different past. If it had been different, maybe she wouldn't have been here right now. And no matter how this turned out, she wouldn't have missed these past few days for the world.

"Now who's thinking too hard?" Shaw's warm breath circled around her ear and cheek, causing an army of goose bumps to suddenly rise up and march down along her arms and spine.

She realized that she'd let her thoughts drift too far. "What?"

In reply, he lightly slid his finger over the ridge just above her eyebrows. There was a furrow there, just as there had been on his forehead. She laughed in response, the sound filtering through him. Making him feel as if, when he wasn't looking, sunshine had somehow sneaked into his system.

Andrew smiled to himself. Looked as if another one of his kids was about to fall, he thought. And if Shaw wasn't, if for some reason his son clung to that damn perch of his, he promised himself to give Shaw a little helpful push over the edge. Because as sure as he was standing here, watching his family, Andrew could see that there was more than a little something going on between his oldest and Moira McCormick.

The same kind of crackling electricity that had gone on between him and Rose.

The same kind, he promised himself, that would go on again once she fully returned to him.

"Seconds, anyone?" he asked, then smiled at the sea of hands that went up.

"You've got to be tired," Shaw protested.

Unable to help himself, Shaw had driven over to Moira's hotel after his shift was over, then lingered in the one restaurant that had an unobstructed view of the hotel's entrance. Waiting for her. Needing just to see her while he still could.

When Moira had looked in his direction after he'd called to her, her face had broken out in a wreath of smiles. He told himself that was enough, but somehow, he couldn't get his feet to move in the direction of the exit. Instead, he'd invited her for a late supper.

She'd countered with an invitation to her room, adding in a seductively lowered voice that Carrie was now staying in her own room at the hotel.

He'd countered the invitation by making an assessment of her condition.

Tired? She'd looked surprised at his question. "Is that your way of saying you don't want to see me?"

"No, that's my way of saying that you've been up since four, filming until way after dark and, according to what you told me, you've got lines to memorize for tomorrow." Even if she hadn't told him, he knew her schedule cold. Knew with reasonable certainty what she was doing almost every hour of the day. He told himself it was his way of coping. "Shouldn't you be in bed?"

Even in the restaurant's dim light, he could see her eyes shining with amusement. "I thought you'd never ask."

They walked toward the elevators. A car stood open, waiting for them. He ushered her in quickly, wanting to ride up to her room without someone else coming along with them.

"That wasn't a proposition."

The doors closed. She pretended to look serious. "Someone else caught your eye?"

He only smiled. "Not possible when I'm blinded by the light you cast."

Only training kept her from letting her mouth drop open. The elevator stopped on her floor. She was hardly aware of walking out and toward her room.

"My God, Shaw, that's positively poetic. Who fed you the line?"

They stopped before her door. He waited as she opened the door, anticipation elbowing its way to the fore.

"Something I remember reading once," he admitted. Then he added quietly, "It didn't really make any sense to me, until I met you."

"You're just getting better and better at this." She could feel herself choking up as she closed the door behind them. It took effort not to give way to her emotions. She'd known him such a short time, how could he have such an effect on her? The heart knows what it wants, something whispered inside of her. Too bad the heart was eventually going to be disappointed, she thought sadly.

"Tell me more."

He wasn't much on poetry, and venturing out on a limb, telling her what he felt, was a little more reckless than he wanted to be right now. "Sorry, fresh out."

There was only one light on in the suite. She didn't bother putting on any more. "Okay, then show me."

Her voice, low, seductive, wound itself around him. "Are you sure you're not tired?"

She grinned, suddenly feeling alive and vital. "I guess I'm just going to have to show you how not tired I am."

Before he could protest or do what he knew in his heart was the right thing, she was weaving that magic of hers all about him. First her arms went around his neck, then her body pressed against his, the heat issuing an invitation of its own.

The second her mouth touched his, he could feel the fireworks going off, feel the desire growing. Feel, too, the sadness that stood off in the wings, promising itself to him the moment she left town.

He tried to shut its presence out, but couldn't.

Its mere existence urged him on, had him determined to make love with her more enthusiastically than he had up until now. It encouraged him to take advantage of his time a little more zealously.

And all the while, pretend that tomorrow, with all its emptiness, would not come.

He made love to her as if it were their last time.

And their first.

Exhilarated, Moira sank down in her chair. They were filming in the heart of Aurora's uptown district and the weather was cooperating beautifully. The scene had been a tough one to nail down, but she had gotten it in one overwhelming take. Her energy was flying so high, she'd funneled it all into her character, made the words come out just right at the pivotal moment. The second the director had called, "Cut—print," the rest of the cast and crew had burst into a round of applause she found both humbling and energizing, as well.

Murmuring her thanks, she'd retreated off camera to her chair.

Slowly, her surroundings came back into focus. She was Moira again instead of Sally, her character in the movie. And as Moira, she became aware of all the things that mattered to Moira. The police personnel she'd prevailed upon the director to take on as extras were all gathered together, exchanging nervous talk and laughter until the cameras started rolling again. She saw Amy tugging at the hem of a too-short skirt. The girl was playing what she no longer was and doing a fine job of it.

Moira smiled to herself. She had her doubts that Amy was as old as she claimed, but there was no way to prove the girl wrong. According to Shaw, there was no missing child posting on her on the Internet, no record of her anywhere, not under the name she had given them. Her fingerprints hadn't shown up in the database, either.

Maybe someday she'd get the girl to trust her enough to tell her who she really was, she mused. But right now, since the girl appeared to have no home other than the broken-down motel room she'd first taken her to, Moira fully intended to take Amy back with her when she returned to Los Angeles.

She was confident that with her connections, she could always find work for her until Amy finally decided what she wanted to do with her life.

The same went for Carrie.

Looking to the side, she saw her sister in the distance, talking to a stuntman. Laughing. God, but it was good to see Carrie laugh again. Simon had left town and Carrie was beginning to revert to her old self again. There was no doubt in her mind that her sister would remain with her until after the baby was born.

And for as long as she wanted after that.

Moira looked down at her nails, checking to see if she'd broken one in the last scene.

If she was busy getting immersed in other people's lives, maybe she wouldn't notice that her own was going to be empty all too soon.

She thought of Shaw. The way she did at least a hundred times a day.

"How do you do it?"

Moira jumped. It was as if she'd just conjured up his voice. Composing herself, she looked over her shoulder just as he walked up to her.

"What are you doing here?" Reese was right behind him, looking around. He clearly looked as if he wanted to remain.

With the unconscious familiarity of a lover, Shaw lightly laid his hand on her shoulder. "I'm actually here on official business," he told her, "but you were busy, so I decided to wait." Before she could ask what kind of official business he could have with her, he said, "That scene you just did had nothing to do with the last one."

"All movies are shot out of sequence," she told him. "They're trying to make use of the locale, so we're shooting all the scenes in front of City Hall today." She nodded at the ivy-covered building that had been standing for over ninety years.

He and Reese had come on the set just as she'd ended one scene and then launched into the last one. "How can you hop around like that? It'd take me all day to build up to what you just did."

Reese laughed. "It'd take him all year and he would still sound like someone had done a lobotomy on him just before he opened his mouth."

Moira laughed as she rose from the folding chair. "So, what did you come to tell me?"

Shaw scanned the area until he found who he was looking for. It had been one of those days that made him glad he'd chosen the career he had. "Actually, we came to tell Amy she doesn't have to be afraid anymore."

Moira made the connection instantly. "You caught the guy behind the prostitution ring?"

The last tip he and Reese had followed up on had paid off. "Got enough on him to put him and the people in his organization away for a long, long time. She doesn't have to be afraid anymore," he repeated. "When the time comes, we are going to need her to testify, though."

Moira nodded. He wasn't telling her anything she hadn't expected. "She won't be hard to find," she told him. "She'll be staying with me."

Shaw assumed she was talking about the hotel. "This isn't going to be for a while. The law moves a hell of a lot slower than any of us would like. I'm talking about after the movie's made."

The hairdresser came to fuss over her hair, but Moira put her hand up to stop him. "Give me a few minutes." She knew Shaw would want to talk to her in relative privacy. The hairdresser stepped back. "So am I," she told Shaw.

"So what, you're adopting her?"

"Giving her a job. As my assistant."

He saw Carrie standing off on the side. "And your sister?"

"She's my stand-in."

Just how far did her largesse extend? "Even when you're not filming?"

"Then she's my sister." He came from a big family; he knew how it worked. "Carrie can stay with me for as long as she wants to."

"I didn't know you ran a day care."

"I don't." Was he trying to pick a fight with her? Why? They had so little time left together. Why was he trying to spoil it? "It's called family. Ask your dad about it."

"Amy's not your family," he pointed out.

"Amy needs a family. Besides, I like her. She's

a great kid. Nobody ever took the time to notice, that's all."

It wasn't working. He was trying to find a way to push her away and all he'd succeeded in doing was wanting her more. Wanting her with a swiftness that took his breath away. Wanting her because she made his heart swell for so many different reasons.

Although Reese had stepped back to give them a little privacy, it wasn't enough. He leaned in to her, lowering his voice. "When can you get away?"

Her eyes twinkled. She looked toward her trailer parked over in the distance. "I've got a lunch break coming up."

"Might not be long enough." Not for what he had in mind.

"Hey," she kidded, "I'm the star. They'll cut me a little slack." It was all she could do not to wind her arms around his neck, but she knew he'd hate having an audience observe them.

That he was tempted showed him just how much this woman affected him. "I'm on duty."

She sighed. "I know. But there's always tonight. We can run lines." She looked at him significantly. "Or anything else you want."

What he wanted was for the interlude not to end. For her not to return back to Los Angeles. For her not to leave his life.

The realization didn't really startle him. He'd felt it creeping into his consciousness for a while now. It was just not something he allowed himself to readily admit. "Sounds like a plan to me." He looked back to where Amy had been standing a moment ago, but the girl was gone. "Now, where can I find Amy?"

"C'mon," she told him, "we'll find her together."

Together. It had a nice ring to it. He knew he was deluding himself, something he never did, but he did like the sound of that.

Together.

Being together with her.

But because his mother had disappeared out of his life so suddenly, he'd grown up believing that nothing was permanent. And this certainly was no different. He'd enjoy the moment—what he had—and when it was over, when it was behind him, he'd move on. Everyone in life moved on. They did that or they died. There was no other choice.

Chapter Fourteen

Even as Claire approached the tub with its bright, Wedgwood-blue tile, a feeling of dread descended over her. It was the same every morning. A cold iciness would pass up and down her spine at the very thought of what lay ahead of her.

She didn't like water. Never went to the beach, never took those long, luxurious baths other women raved about. To her, the sight of water in anything other than a glass or shallow pot instantly brought fear with it. Claire knew her phobia was unreasonable, bordering on the insane, but it was something she had never been able to conquer.

Faced with a body of water, she always saw her own death.

Unable to come to grips with her pathological fear, Claire worked around it. She washed her face with a washcloth and took showers. Quick ones with the showerhead aimed low because she particularly didn't like getting any water on her face.

Washing her hair always presented a challenge. She did it in the sink, where she could control the flow and the direction of the water.

Claire shed her robe. Taking a deep breath, she stepped into the bathtub, then closed the sliding door behind her.

The feeling of being trapped immediately hovered over her.

Bracing herself, she went to move the showerhead downward. It wouldn't budge. Someone had returned it to its original position and now it resisted being moved. She tried it again, but it was stuck. Muttering under her breath, Claire pushed against the metal until the head bent down again.

Three minutes, just three minutes, that's all she needed.

Mind over matter, Claire projected herself three minutes into the future, then turned the faucet on.

Standing in the kitchen, about to start preparing breakfast, Andrew looked up at the ceiling. The floor above his head had creaked and then he heard the sound of the sliding glass door being closed.

She was up, he thought. That meant she'd be down for breakfast soon.

This morning, the house was empty except for him and Rose, or Claire, as she called herself. Just like in the very beginning, he thought with a sad smile. Neither Rayne nor Teri had come home last night. Rayne was out on an all-night stakeout and Teri was spending the night at Callie's place. The two were going over wedding plans.

Weddings. He shook his head, smiling. Without comparing notes, it turned out that all four of his children's weddings were clustered together in the same month. When he'd found out, he'd made the suggestion that they all take place on the same day. He'd gotten summarily shot down, only to have the idea resurrected again shortly thereafter.

Consequently, Callie and Brent, Clay and Ilene, Rayne and Cole and Teri and Hawk were all getting married in a month.

A month.

He wondered if Rose would still be here then. She'd mentioned two months when she came, but yesterday, she'd said something about having to return up north to her job. To her life.

The taste of bitterness filled his mouth. Her life was here, with their children.

With him.

But so far, there was no way he could get her to see that.

Because she was still Claire and not Rose.

Brian had told him he might have to get used to his wife's condition. He knew his younger brother was just trying to be helpful, but he didn't want to think about that. Didn't want to try to make peace with the idea that she would never be the woman he loved. Never be Rose again.

And then, because the realist coexisted with the idealist, Andrew paused, thinking.

Maybe he should try to build a new life with this stranger he'd discovered living in Rose's body. Because he knew in his heart that his Rose was still in there somewhere. He could hear Rose in the way Claire laughed, could see her in Claire's eyes. And whether she answered to "Claire" or "Rose," she still had that endearing tilt of the head when she was pondering on something.

If he could just get her to love him again, no matter what name she answered to, then maybe—

Andrew stiffened, the first of the eggs he was about to break over the bowl falling from his fingers to the counter.

He heard a scream.

The sound carried through the vent, seeming to vibrate through the very floor. The water was running and Rose was screaming.

Andrew broke into a run.

He didn't even stop to think, to try to figure out what was going on. He was on the stairs in a moment, flying up them two at a time.

In less than a heartbeat, not standing on ceremony, he'd rushed into Callie's old bedroom.

The bathroom door was closed. As he tried it, he found it locked.

"Rose, are you in there?" He pounded on the door when she made no answer. "Rose, what's wrong?"

She was still screaming. The sound curdled his blood.

Andrew put his shoulder to the door and hit it as hard as he could. The simple lock gave, splintering the jamb as the door flew open. The next instant, he flung open the sliding door and pulled her out. She screamed and gasped for air.

There was water everywhere. The showerhead had somehow broken off and water sprayed the entire room. Andrew was soaked in an instant.

With one arm wrapped protectively around Claire, he reached into the tub and shut off the water. Water dripped into his eyes. She was shaking like a leaf. Andrew grabbed a towel from the rack and wrapped it around her as best he could, then took the second towel and threw it over her shoulders.

Claire stopped screaming. Instead, she began to sob uncontrollably. Not knowing what else to do, Andrew sat down on the closed commode and took her onto his lap. Holding her, he began to rock to and fro, trying as best as he knew how to soothe her.

"It's all right, you're safe now. Just an old showerhead coming apart, that's all, nothing more.'' Andrew had no idea what had gone on in her head, only that he'd never seen the kind of fear he'd glimpsed on her face when he'd pulled her out.

Very gently, he took the edge of one of the towels and wiped her cheeks.

He knew all about her phobia. She'd admitted it to him the first day she'd arrived at the house. He had given her a tour of the house and pointed out the remodeled bathroom, telling her that she'd have exclusive use of it during her stay. When he'd gone on to show her Teri's cache of bubble bath crystals, she'd told him she'd have no use for them.

''I only take showers,'' she told him quietly. ''Quick ones. I hate getting water on my face.''

It didn't take a brain surgeon to know why. He'd figured it had to do with the car going over the side and into the river. But the look in her eyes when he began to say as much had him holding his tongue. Instincts told him not to push it, so he'd retreated.

He resisted the urge to tighten his arms around her now. To hold her the way a man held the woman he loved. Instead, he held her as if she were a child, to be protected and comforted.

''I'm sorry about that, Claire. Really sorry. I'll put a new one in right away. Maybe I should have a plumber put it in because I'm not overly handy when it comes to this kind of stuff. I—''

He stopped abruptly as she turned her head up to his. There was this look in her eyes he couldn't begin to fathom. It was wild, and yet somehow centered, as if she were struggling to focus on something.

"Rose," she whispered.

She'd said the name so softly, he wasn't certain that he had heard her correctly. Thought that maybe it was just his heart speaking. "What?"

She swallowed, her throat sore, her voice hoarse. Tears felt as if they were gathering inside her entire body.

"Rose," she repeated. "My name is Rose." And then tears spilled out onto her already-dampened cheeks. "I remember. Oh, my God, I remember." She covered her mouth with her hands, afraid that she would begin sobbing again. All sorts of emotions scrambled through her. "Andrew, I remember. I know who you are. I know where I am."

How long had he dreamed about this? Hoped for this? He was afraid to believe it was true.

"Are you sure?" Andrew held her by her shoulders, anchoring her in place. "Oh, God, Rose, you remember?"

Stifling another sob, she nodded. Words began to flow from her lips as quickly as the water had from the pipe when the shower head broke off.

"Everything." To prove it, she began to recite the events of the last day that she had been Rose Cavanaugh, excitement building in her voice. "The car, it went over the side. The door was stuck, I couldn't get it to open. You know how you always had me lock the doors whenever I drove the car. It went into the water. I thought I was going to die there.

"And then I finally got it open, but I was so far down in the water, I didn't think I could make it back up to the top. I thought I was going to drown." She blinked, trying to put the kaleidoscope of events swirling through her brain in order. "But I must have gotten out somehow." She looked at him, shaking her head. "I guess I just blacked out. Someone stopped to pick me up. He drove me somewhere and then tried to…tried to…"

"Don't." Andrew knew this was too much for her. He didn't want her handling the ordeal in her fragile state of mind.

But she shook her head, doggedly continuing. "He tried to rape me. I managed to get away before he could." She closed her eyes, gathering the memories together. "I remember walking, just walking. I was cold and wet and scared and I didn't know who I was."

And then she opened her eyes again, looking at him. Everything finally made sense after all these years. "I must have walked all the way to Lucy's diner. She came running out when she saw me through the window. Lucy and her husband took me in. I remember being sick."

He listened, wanting to interrupt in a dozen places, knowing he couldn't. She needed to get this all out at once. So she could finally put it behind her.

"Lucy found me a place to stay and gave me a job." A fondness entered Rose's voice. The pair were the only two people she allowed into her life in all this time. "She and her husband have been very good to me."

Choked with emotion, Andrew felt as if his throat would close up. He'd come so very close to losing her. Too close.

"Remind me to thank them."

She looked at him, seeing him perhaps for the first time, this man who had loved her all these long years. "You never gave up hope, did you?"

"Never." Still holding her on his lap, he closed his arms around her. "Everyone tried to tell me that the evidence all pointed to your body being washed out to sea. I didn't care about the evidence. In my heart, I knew you were out there somewhere. And that I had to find you."

She felt as if a huge weight had been lifted from her. As if she were a bird that was allowed to fly again after being tethered for such an extremely long period of time.

"Oh, God, Andrew, I'm so glad to be home." Fresh tears filled her eyes. "I've missed you. Even when I didn't know it was you I was missing, I missed you. There was always a piece of me that wasn't there." And then, along with her memory came the reason for the argument that led to her departure in the first place. "You have to know that Mike and I never—"

Andrew placed a finger against her lips, silencing whatever was to follow. She didn't need to say it. He didn't need to hear it.

Love and gratitude filled every available space within him.

"I know. And even if you had, it doesn't matter. Do you understand? It doesn't matter. Looking for you these past fifteen years has taught me what really counts and what doesn't. And all that counts is having you home again."

Unable to contain her emotions any longer, Rose wrapped her arms around his neck and kissed him, kissed the man who had moved heaven and earth to find her when she'd been so lost.

Kissed the husband she'd loved since the beginning of time.

Moira looked on at the vast collection of people milling around in Andrew Cavanaugh's backyard. She'd been to bigger parties. Despite the fact that there were people in the house, as well as outside, and that Teri had confided to her that practically the entire Aurora police force, active and retired, along with their families were in attendance, she had been at affairs where this party could have easily been tucked into a small corner.

But Moira knew without being told that she'd

never attended anything that was remotely happier in nature.

No, she mused, taking a sip of her wine, not even that last Oscar party, the one where the best actress had gushed on for almost ten minutes to any and all who had the misfortune of crossing her path. That had been stylized happiness.

This was quite different in nature. It was without pretense. Just plain, unadulterated joy. It made her happy just to be here, just to share the unabashed emotion that hummed throughout the area.

She looked around for Shaw. He kept being drawn away, but she spotted him and made her way over.

"Thanks for inviting me," she said when she finally reached him.

He looked up, as if he was surprised she'd found him. Shaw shrugged carelessly at her words. "Can't take exclusive credit for this. It was really my father's idea."

"And you wouldn't have if he hadn't told you to?"

From where she was standing, there was no other way to interpret his words. What was going on? They'd made love just last night, as they had every night while she'd been filming here. But this afternoon, he was acting as if being around her was putting him out.

He looked annoyed at her question. "I thought you might have better things to do."

"Something better than witnessing joy up close and personal?" she asked incredulously, looking back at the guest of honor. Rose Cavanaugh stood beside her husband. The two looked more like newlyweds than a couple that had been married over thirty-three years. "I don't think so."

Shaw frowned. "You're getting ready to leave tomorrow," he reminded her.

She was more than aware of that and more than a little sad about the prospect. She didn't want to leave. Not this town, which contained memories for her of a happier time in her youth, not this family whom she was just getting to know and like—and not this man, who remained a puzzle to her but one whose pieces she wanted to reexamine at length.

"That's tomorrow," she told him. "Today is today and I like living each day one day at a time."

He was doing his damnedest to distance himself from her, from the inevitable, and he wished she'd let him get on with it. "Nice motto."

The words had a sarcastic bite. Struggling against their sting, Moira forced herself to make allowances for his mood. She knew Shaw had to be going through a lot himself, what with his mother finally regaining her memory and finally returning to them in every sense of the word.

But still, what he said hurt.

She searched for a way to lighten the unspoken tension between them. "You know, when they make the movie version of this, I think I'd like to play your mother.''

Preoccupied, looking for an excuse to get away from her again, Shaw looked at her. ''What?''

She supposed it was more her profession than her nature that made her see things in a certain light.

''Well, this has all the markings of a wonderful, feel-good movie.'' She spread her hands out before her as if projecting a story on the screen. ''Woman disappears, is presumed dead by everyone except for her loving husband who never gives up hope that she's alive somewhere. And then he actually finds her. A winner at the box office every time.''

''Don't forget my part,'' Rayne interjected, coming up behind them. ''If I hadn't stopped by that diner a couple of months ago, on the way to question a witness, none of this would have happened.''

''We also have to give star billing to the showerhead,'' Callie teased, coming up on the other side of them. One look at her face told Moira just how elated Callie was. But family never missed an opportunity to tease one another. ''If it hadn't come off and sprayed water in Mom's face, her memory might never have returned and we wouldn't have our happy ending.''

Listening, Moira shook her head. ''It's amazing how life's little coincidences dovetail together to make things happen.''

''Yeah, amazing,'' Shaw echoed, edging away.

He spared Moira a glance. ''If you'll excuse me, there's someone I need to talk to.''

Before she could say anything, he'd walked off.

Feeling a little awkward, she looked at Rayne. ''Is it me, or is there a chill in the air?''

''Yes,'' Rayne confirmed, then elaborated. ''There's a chill in the air and it's you.''

Well, that certainly made things no clearer. ''Excuse me?''

Rayne paused to pick up one of the hors d'oeuvres her father had made. Fueled by triumph, he had handled every aspect of this quickly thrown together celebration and still managed to outdo himself. ''Shaw doesn't want you leaving.''

She had strong doubts about that. ''Well, he has a funny way of showing it. I would have said that he couldn't wait for me to be gone.''

''Then you would have been wrong,'' Rayne told her simply. ''Shaw doesn't wear his heart on his sleeve, but we've got him pretty well figured out by now. You've rocked his world when he didn't want it rocked.''

Moira was certain that the other woman was just trying to be polite and make her feel good. ''And you've figured this out how?''

''Trust me, a sister knows.'' In a gesture filled with acceptance and camaraderie, Rayne slipped her arm around her. ''He won't admit it, but he and I got pretty close when he was trying to save me.''

Okay, Moira thought, she was lost again. "Trying to save you?"

Popping the rest of the hors d'oeuvre into her mouth, she grinned.

"I was an A-number-one pain in the butt growing up. I blamed Dad for Mom's disappearance and in short made life a living hell for him and the others. Shaw spent a lot of time trying to straighten me out." The grin faded a little as she became serious. "That's the kind of guy Shaw is. When he loves someone, he loves them completely, come hell or high water."

Moira felt as if she were intruding into something personal. "Why are you telling me all this?"

"Because I know him and I know he has feelings for you. Deep feelings." She picked up one more hors d'oeuvre, then paused as if studying it. She raised her eyes to Moira's face. "The two of you are going to have to work this out for yourselves, but if you hurt him," she added, "I'll come after you."

"Thanks for the warning."

"Don't mention it."

Rayne was wrong, Moira thought as the other woman walked off to rejoin her fiancé. If Shaw cared, she'd know. Somehow, a part of her would know. And right now, he was freezing her out. Freezing her out so badly that it hurt. Yes, he'd extended his father's invitation to her, but grudgingly so.

And he had made himself fairly scarce throughout the party, acting as if she were already gone, instead of making the most of the time they had left.

You didn't do that if you cared about a person.

With a sigh, she turned away. And spotted Shaw. He was talking to a woman she didn't recognize. The woman was laughing at something he'd just said and she draped her arm around him. Possessively. Shaw made no effort to step away.

Moira felt something squeeze inside of her.

She looked around for her sister. It was time to go.

Chapter Fifteen

Moira looked at her watch. It was almost time to leave for the airport. Carrie had already called from her room, saying that she and Amy were ready and just waiting on her.

And she was waiting on Shaw.

All morning long, she'd felt as if she'd been holding her breath. He knew she was leaving today, so where was he?

He's not coming.

Moira shut the voice out of her head, even though she knew she should be paying more attention to it. But there were some lessons that were not easily learned.

Returning from the party last night, she'd spent the remainder of the evening waiting for Shaw to call. Hoping he would show up at her door.

But he hadn't.

The rest of the night had dragged by, one microsecond at a time, until it was finally behind her and dawn was poking its way into the world. Amassing maybe fifty minutes' worth of sleep over the course of the entire night, she felt like hell.

That's what you get for putting your faith in the old shell game, she upbraided herself as she'd artfully applied makeup to hide the dark circles under her eyes. Except, instead of a pea, you stuck love under one of those shells. Love, love, who's got the love?

Certainly not Shaw.

She'd thrown down her eye shadow wand. It had bounced off the counter, leaving a light blue streak as it fell to the floor. Anger coupled with frustration as she bent to pick it up again. What had she been for him? A fling? A celebrity tryst?

She knew she wasn't being entirely fair to Shaw, but she didn't much feel like being fair. Not when her heart was aching so badly.

The moment she heard the knock on her door, she flew to it and flung it open, ready to forgive and forget because he had come.

She struggled very hard not to let her smile fall when she saw that it was Reese standing on her doorstep and not Shaw.

"Hi." She gestured him into the room. "Come to say goodbye?"

Reese looked uncomfortable as he entered the suite. His customary easygoing smile looked just a trifle forced. But there was a look of compassion in his eyes when he turned to look at her. It was clear he didn't regard her as a movie star any longer, but someone who was real, with real feelings.

"Yeah." He ran his hand along his stubble, nervous, looking for words. "I wanted you to know that I really liked having you as a ride-along. And I appreciate that bit part—"

"Walk-on." The correction was automatic. She'd even seen to it that he'd had two lines to recite and to his credit, he'd done them well.

"Yeah, that." He beamed, relaxing. "I appreciate the chance. It was a real kick."

"Well, I enjoyed riding along with you. And I did learn a lot." *Maybe a little more than I'd bargained for,* she added silently. "You can tell Shaw that for me when you see him."

"Sure, I'll do that." Reese shifted slightly. They both knew they were ignoring the elephant in the living room. He shoved his hands into his pockets, looking down at her packed bags. "Um, he asked me to say goodbye for him."

Well, that settled it. Shaw wasn't coming. "He needs a ventriloquist?"

Reese blew out a breath, shaking his head. "Ask

me, my partner needs to have his head examined. But nobody asked me.''

Moira smiled, understanding what the detective wasn't saying and appreciating the silent message. She brushed a kiss against his stubbled cheek. ''Maybe not, but it's nice to hear, anyway.'' She stepped back to look at Reese. ''Thank you.''

He shrugged, as if his words were the least he could say and they both knew it. ''Got anything you want me to tell him?''

There was a great deal she wanted to say to Shaw, but not through a go-between. Besides, what was the use? Shaw had said it all by not coming to see her off. By not calling to try to make arrangements to see her again once this movie was under wraps.

She shook her head. ''Just goodbye, I guess. There doesn't seem to be anything else to say.''

Reese looked genuinely disappointed. ''If I should ever get down to L.A.—'' he began.

''I'd be hurt if you didn't look me up. Call me anytime.'' Pulling a hotel pad over to her, Moira wrote down her private number as well as her cell number and her address. She tore off the sheet, then folded it in half and handed it to him. ''Here. Just make sure this doesn't fall into the wrong hands and wind up on eBay.''

Taking out his wallet, Reese tucked the piece of paper behind several bills. ''Not a chance.'' Pocketing it again, he glanced toward the door. ''Well, I guess I'd better get going.''

Hooking her arm through his, she walked him to the door.

"Go catch some bad guys," she told him fondly.

It wasn't until she'd closed the door again and was fairly certain that Reese had made his way down the hall to the elevator that she let the tears fall.

She allowed herself exactly three minutes of self-pity. Then, squaring her shoulders, Moira picked up the telephone to call her sister. There was a plane to catch. And the rest of her life to live.

"So, you're not going to ask?"

Reese had spent the better part of the afternoon glaring at him, both in the office and in the car. So far, he'd done a fair job of ignoring the man. It hadn't been easy.

Shaw gripped the steering wheel, knowing he couldn't avoid the topic any longer. "Ask what?"

Annoyed, Reese blew out a long breath. "What Moira said."

Shaw stared straight ahead at the road before him. Traffic was light. "All right. What did she say?"

"She said goodbye."

Prepared to hear more, Shaw was surprised by the economy of words. It proved his point, that this was just an interlude for the actress and that he was right when he felt he couldn't make anything of it. Being right didn't make him happy.

"That's it?"

"Well, what did you expect her to say?" From Reese's tone it was clear to Shaw that his partner had taken sides and it wasn't with him. "That's all you said and that wasn't even in person."

"What do you want from me?"

Reese lost his patience. "I want you to stop being an idiot, that's what I want. A gorgeous woman like that doesn't come along every day."

Well, at least they were agreed on that. "No, she doesn't." Shaw set his mouth grimly. "And now she's back where she belongs." He could feel Reese's eyes as he stared at him.

"How do you know where she belongs?"

What, did Reese need a road map? It was as plain as the nose on his face. "She's an actress."

"So she belongs in Hollywood?" Reese hooted. "You never heard of airplanes? People commute all the time. And not all the so-called 'stars' live within walking distance of the studio, buddy. Los Angeles isn't exactly at the end of the known world. You might think about paying her a visit sometime."

Yeah, right, Shaw thought. Like some starstruck groupie who was fixated on her. "What, go stand in front of her studio in hopes she'd turn up?"

Reese shook his head in complete amazement. "You know, for a smart man, you have absolutely no imagination."

Shaw glanced at him as he came to a stop at a light. Reese pulled out his wallet, took a piece of paper out of it and then, leaning over, tucked that into the top pocket of Shaw's jacket.

The light turned green. Shaw didn't have time to fish out the paper and look at it. ''What's that?''

''Her address and phone number.''

''She gave it to you?'' Why would she give it to Reese and not him? But then, he hadn't asked for it, Shaw reminded himself. Knowing Reese, his partner had probably broadly hinted.

Reese nodded. ''Said if I was ever in the area, to look her up.''

Annoyed, Shaw pulled out the paper and held it out to his partner. ''So, then, this is yours.''

Reese pushed his hand away. ''Damn it, Shaw, don't be so obtuse. Moira meant that information for you, not me. Except you weren't there to give it to, like you should have been.''

For the time being, Shaw replaced the paper in his pocket. But there was no sense in keeping it. It wasn't as if he was going to act on the information there. He didn't belong in L.A. any more than she belonged in Aurora. It was just something he was going to have to come to terms with—if everybody else would let him. ''We're from two different worlds, Reese.''

''That's a crock.'' He looked at him sharply, but Reese remained unfazed. ''You're both earthlings. I figure that's a good start.''

''Not good enough.''

Reese sighed, temporarily giving up. "Never figured you to be a dumb man, Shaw."

Shaw said nothing.

But he left the paper in his pocket.

"What's this?"

Shaw looked at the small envelope his father handed him. It had been two weeks since Moira and the production company had left Aurora. The excitement of having a major film crew in their midst was just beginning to dissipate around the city, but Shaw found that his own restlessness was increasing instead of lessening. The only thing that was lessening these days was his patience. With himself and with others.

In an effort to steer his life back onto familiar grounds, he'd stopped by his father's house to spend a little time with the family. But they only succeeded in irritating him, the way everything and everyone had ever since she'd left.

The house had all but cleared out right after dinner and he'd gone out on the patio to get some air and maybe some perspective. All he found was air.

When his father came out to join him, Shaw searched his mind for a scrap of conversation and came up empty. So he'd stood, facing the back of the yard, and let his father take the lead.

Andrew surprised him by placing the small envelope into his hand.

"An open-end round-trip ticket," Andrew told him.

Shaw didn't open the envelope. "To where?" he asked suspiciously.

"L.A.," his father replied matter-of-factly. "Where you go from there once the plane lands is your own business."

He knew where this was leading. He held the envelope out to his father, but Andrew made no effort to take it back. "I'm not going to see her."

Andrew nodded. "Fair enough." He sat down at the table, motioning for Shaw to join him. After a beat, his son did. "But I think you should know that the same people who chipped in for this ticket took an oath to kill you if you didn't use it." Andrew grinned when his son looked at him. "That's even coming from Callie who's always been in your corner."

Shaw turned the envelope around in his hand. "Kill me, huh?"

"That's what they said."

Shaw sighed, then rose to his feet as he pocketed the ticket. "Maybe I'd better think about it, then."

"Maybe." Andrew watched his oldest as he headed for the patio door. "I'd think fast if I were you."

Shaw stopped and looked at him. "Why?"

Andrew took a long sip of his lemonade, then said, "The ticket's for tomorrow."

"Tomorrow?" Shaw echoed incredulously. That

wasn't enough time to get things squared away. "I haven't cleared—"

Andrew knew what his son was going to say before the words were out of his mouth. He'd gone to Shaw's superior and put in for some vacation time for his son. "Already taken care of."

Shaw laughed as he shook his head. He might have known. "You don't leave much to chance, do you?"

"Never get ahead that way." He grinned. "Tell her hi for all of us."

Shaw had his doubts about the venture. After all, he hadn't even stopped by to tell her goodbye. He was acutely aware that they hadn't parted on the best of terms. "She might not want to see me."

Andrew met his son's eyes. "You'll never find out standing here, will you?"

"Guess not." Opening the sliding glass door, Shaw went inside.

Andrew silently toasted him with his lemonade glass. "Smart boy."

Moira let herself into the house, flipping on the light switch beside the security keypad.

Tired, it took her a minute to remember the code and re-arm it. Tossing her key on the side table, she shed her purse and stepped out of her shoes as she made her way to the living room sofa. She fell into it, wilting, trying to gather enough energy together to make it up the stairs to her bedroom.

She felt beyond drained.

It was late. She'd remained on the set today longer than usual, running lines for the next day with Carrie.

Thoughts of her sister made her smile. At least things were going well there. Carrie had really come into her own these past couple of weeks. After a few days here, she'd insisted on moving out and getting her own apartment. It was time, Carrie had told her, trying to assuage her big-sister concerns, to start standing on her own two feet again. She'd even taken to mentoring Amy, who showed a great deal of promise now that there were people taking an interest in her as a human being.

The part of Moira that wasn't bent on mothering every creature that breathed, especially her own blood, was extremely proud of Carrie.

Moira moodily dragged a hand through her hair. She wished she could be that resilient.

It felt as if the spring that governed her ability to bounce back had rusted in place. Temporarily, she insisted silently as she debated just sacking out on the sofa instead of making the long trip up to her room.

For now, she was trying to fill up every waking moment in her life with work or something connected to work. If she had no time to think, she couldn't hurt, right?

It was a good theory, but the hurt came anyway, when she least expected it. Like some giant, macabre jack-in-the-box clown, leaping up at her and taking her breath away. Stripping a little more of her heart.

Moira frowned in disgust. She'd never, ever thought she could fall in love so fast, so hard and be so wrong about it.

But she'd obviously been wrong about Shaw Cavanaugh because if she hadn't been, he would have come to her that last day. He would have tried to make some kind of arrangements to see her, to at least stay in touch. Reese had found the time; why hadn't Shaw, instead of just letting her go like that?

It'd been miserably long two weeks and there hadn't been a phone call, a letter, a carrier pigeon with a note strapped to its leg, nothing. Not even so much as a telltale hang-up on her machine. She'd given her numbers to Reese and she was positive that the man had understood that she'd meant them for Shaw. She would have bet anything that Reese had given Shaw the number to her cell and her house. If she wasn't hearing from Shaw it was because he didn't want to call her.

Didn't want to see her.

Didn't want her.

Eventually, she told herself, closing her eyes to keep the tears from coming again, that was going to sink in. But not now.

Moira opened her eyes and sighed. She couldn't go on moping like this, like one half of some tragic star-crossed lovers' duo. It had to stop, here and now. Before she lost any more weight and became a walking advertisement for matches.

What she needed, she decided, was a long, hot soothing bath. And a sandwich.

The doorbell rang just as she'd finally mustered enough oomph to dig herself out of the soft, enfolding leather of her sofa and get to her feet.

It was almost eleven. Nobody ever called or visited her around this time when she was filming. Something had to be wrong. Thinking of all sorts of scenarios, none of them good, she was at the door in a second, adrenaline making short work of her lack of energy. "Who is it?"

"Open the door, Moira. It's me."

With adrenaline rushing through her, Moira managed to stand absolutely still. Wishful thinking was playing tricks on her mind. On her ears. "Shaw?" she uttered uncertainly.

"Yes."

She didn't remember the code to disarm the alarm. Didn't remember disarming it. Somehow, her fingers followed the pattern they had to hit to keep the siren from going off even as she was yanking on the handle, opening the door.

She stared at him in complete silence, unable to believe he wasn't some figment of her imagination. She'd spent two weeks seeing him everywhere. Her mind had finally gone into overdrive.

Moira was afraid of being disappointed. Again. "What are you doing here?" She waited for him to disappear, to turn into thin air. His molecules didn't rearrange. He was still there.

She wasn't stepping back, wasn't letting him in. After arriving at LAX, he'd spent the better part of the day gathering his nerve together. It had taken him this long to finally come to her house.

Was this a mistake? Had he blown it?

Fear galvanized his spine. He wasn't leaving until he made this right. ''A simple 'Hello, good to see you' would be nice.''

''Hello, good to see you,'' she parroted, still absolutely stunned, still expecting him to vanish. But just in case he was real, she stepped back, opening the door wider. ''What are you doing here?'' she repeated.

He crossed the threshold. Expecting to see opulence, he saw a tastefully decorated living room instead. This could have been anyone's house.

It was *her* house and every nerve ending in his body made him aware of that.

''Seems my family thinks I need to see you.'' He turned around to face her as she closed the door. ''Said they'd be forced to kill me if I didn't.''

For the first time since before she'd left Aurora, she felt a smile entering her being. ''And why would they do that?''

''Because, according to them, I've been a pain in the butt to live with.''

She had a feeling that it had been more strongly voiced than that. ''Oh?''

He felt irritated. Irritated that he was here, irritated that his emotions wouldn't allow him just to back away and be a man. Irritated that he needed her more than he needed air. And every ounce of irritation was evident in his voice.

"Yes, 'oh.' Look, I know this doesn't have a chance in hell of working out—"

Oh, but it does. And you took the first step. You're here. "And why is that?"

He blew out a breath. Was she going to make him draw her a picture? "Because you're a movie star."

Moira cocked her head as if she was fascinated by his reasoning. "And you're prejudiced?"

He couldn't begin to compete, to give her the kind of lifestyle that she was accustomed to. "No, it's just that you're used to better things—"

Shaking her head, she cut him off. "You know, if you've come all this way to try to convince me that you don't want to see me, you could have saved yourself the airfare."

"No, that's just it. I know all the reasons against it, but I still want to see you."

He saw her grinning at him. That grin that promised to undo him and bring him to his knees. "Well, then, I'd say you were going about making your case very badly."

He'd be the first one to agree about that. Talking had never been his best form of communication. "What should I say?"

She laced her fingers through his. ''You could start by telling me how you feel.''

''Like a damn fool.''

Moira laughed. At least he was honest. ''Something a little more romantic than that.''

His tone softened as he caressed her cheek. ''A damn fool who's in love with you.''

Wonderful things were coming in to displace the sadness she'd been forced to live with these past two weeks. ''Better.''

What the hell, he might as well make a clean sweep of it and tell her everything. ''And since you've been gone, I can't seem to concentrate.''

She drew close to him, drawn by the look in his eyes. ''Keep going.''

He wanted her. Not just for now, but forever. Although this second would be nice, too. ''And you'll probably tell me I'm crazy—''

She quickly shook her head, stopping him. ''You're veering off the track again.''

He went for broke, because he couldn't stand tiptoeing around it anymore. If she turned him down, he'd take it like a man and leave.

The hell he would, he realized, looking into her eyes. He was going to wage a campaign, a war, until she gave in. And took him as her willing prisoner.

''Would you tell me I was completely insane if I told you that I wanted to marry you?''

''No.''

The word stood alone, without any embellishments. She was paying him back, he thought. "Is that an answer to my proposal?"

"You haven't proposed yet," she replied simply, struggling to keep her emotions in check when all she wanted to do was throw her arms around his neck and scream, "Yes." "That's an answer to your question about whether or not I thought you were insane." And then she grinned so broadly, she was sure her face was going to crack. "You know, for a man of few words, you're really, really not using them very well."

He slipped his arms around her. The look in her eyes told him he had nothing to fear anymore. "Which ones should I use?"

"Guess."

He said the ones that he'd been carrying around in his heart since she'd left. "Will you marry me?"

"Bingo."

"Is that your answer?"

He couldn't carry off the deadpan. She laughed at the attempt. "No, my answer is yes. Yes, I'll marry you."

And then, because he'd been raised to be the cautious one, he had to give her a way out. "But there's so much to work out."

She knew that. She also knew that they had the most important thing down pat. They loved each other and he'd come to tell her that.

"And we will," she promised. "One detail at a time. Everything's possible with love." Suddenly, she felt lighter than air, even as her body was heating. She rose up on her toes, her body swaying into his. "Let's start out with the honeymoon."

"Sounds good to me."

"See, I knew we were of like minds. Everything else is just secondary."

And as he kissed her, Shaw knew she was right.

* * * * *

Look for Marie's next romance
in Silhouette Special Edition,
coming in August 2004.
Don't miss it!

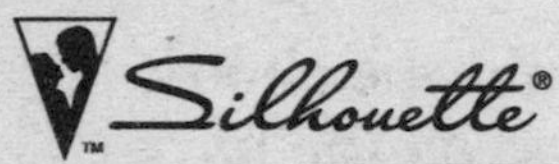

SPECIAL EDITION®

COMING NEXT MONTH

#1621 ROMANCING THE ENEMY—Laurie Paige
The Parks Empire
Nursery school teacher Sara Carlton wanted to uncover the truth surrounding her father's mysterious death years ago, but when she met Cade Parks, the sexy son of the suspected murderer, she couldn't help but expose her heart. Could she shed the shadow of the past and give her love to the enemy?

#1622 HER TEXAS RANGER—Stella Bagwell
Men of the West
When summoned to solve a murder in his hometown, ruggedly handsome Ranger Seth Ketchum stumbled upon high school crush Corrina Dawson. She'd always secretly had her eye on him, too. Then all signs pointed to her father's guilt and suddenly she had to choose one man in her life over the other....

#1623 BABIES IN THE BARGAIN—Victoria Pade
Northbridge Nuptials
After Kira Wentworth's sister was killed, she insisted on taking care of the twin girls left behind. But when she and her sister's husband, Cutty Grant, felt an instant attraction, Kira found herself bargaining for more than just the babies!

#1624 PRODIGAL PRINCE CHARMING—Christine Flynn
The Kendricks of Camelot
Could fairy tales really come true? After wealthy playboy Cord Kendrick destroyed Madison O'Malley's catering truck, he knew he'd have to offer more than money if he wanted to charm his way toward a happy ending. But could he win the heart of his Cinderella without bringing scandal to her door?

#1625 A FOREVER FAMILY—Mary J. Forbes
Suddenly thrust into taking care of his orphaned niece and the family farm, Dr. Michael Rowan needed a helping hand. Luckily his only applicant was kind and loving Shanna McCoy. Close quarters bred a close connection, but only the unexpected could turn these three into a family.

#1626 THE OTHER BROTHER—Janis Reams Hudson
Men of the Cherokee Rose
While growing up, Melanie Pruitt had always been in love with Sloan Chisholm. But when she attended his wedding years later, it was his sexy younger brother Caleb who caught her attention. Both unleashed their passion, then quickly curbed it for the sake of friendship—until Melanie realized that she didn't need another friend, but something more....

SSECNM0604